HELL RAIDERS MC 6

ADEN LOWE

Author's Note: This book contains adult situations and language, violence, and sexual activity. Mature readers only.

Dedicated To:

The memory of Little Orphan Annie, and Lil Bit, two very special little cats who came into my life, and had to leave while this book was being written. I'm not a cat person, but I'm grateful to have had the chance to know these two. When I can, I'll add their stories to my website.

ACKNOWLEDGEMENTS:

I do this to myself every damn time, and choose subject matter that's difficult for me to write. I have a lot of people to thank for getting me through this one, and the things that happened in life while I wrote it.

First, the ladies of the Lowe-Down, you fucking rock. Your constant encouragement and support mean everything to me. I'm proud to call you friends and family.

Ashley, I know I don't always say it, but thank you for all you do. I haven't been easy to work with lately for various reasons, and yet, you're still here. Love you, baby sister.

Elyse, every time I write one of these stories, and the hero is all tortured by knowing he's not good enough for the woman he loves, you know where that comes from. I'm not good enough for you, but I'm eternally grateful you decided to make your life with me.

Tape, thanks for knocking some sense into me a few times. Now I owe you an ass-kicking.

Kenderly Woods, massive thanks for giving Gator his name and backstory!

And most of all, thanks to you, for reading and supporting me and other authors in this wild ride. You can keep up with what I'm doing by following me on Facebook.

I hope you enjoy Crank's Rescue, and that you'll leave a review when you've finished

CHAPTER 1

Crank:

It took every fucking thing I had to keep my bike pointed East, away from Sarah. But I did it. I followed my Brother and his ol' lady back to Stags Leap, and helped them get Tyler and Nicole settled. The whole time, the taste of her lingered in my mouth, and the feel of her slim body pressed against mine haunted me.

I met Sarah when I went to Oklahoma with Fabio to deal with the aftermath of his sister's death. Sarah was the CPS caseworker involved when Alexis and her husband were killed in a traffic accident, and their kids had to be taken care of until Fabio could be found and get there. I wanted her immediately, and knew as soon as I fucked her, I would lose interest. I always did. Until I didn't.

Every single moment turned into torture, and I caved to it. I knew I was being an unbearable bastard, and I did not give one flying fuck. It took three whole days after the return to Stags Leap before one of my Brothers called me on it.

I stomped into the kitchen, mad at the world, intent on coffee, only to find whoever took the last cup failed to start the pot again. A couple of things might have broken during my little tantrum as I refilled everything, but at least the coffee maker survived.

Badger came in from his usual post on the porch, leaned against the counter, and studied me for a long moment. "Who the fuck pissed in your Cheerios, man?"

That took me back a second. "The fuck you talking about?"

The look he gave me said very clearly I had stepped on his last nerve. "Ever since you got back, you've been about as friendly as a buck in rut. And unless I miss my guess, it's the same reason. Pussy done gone to your head."

"Fuck you, old man." Bastard had no business prying into my personal shit.

"Uh huh. Some little Okie chick got you jumping, don't she?" He grinned. "Don't think you're the first fucker around here that's happened to. Still ain't no reason to be all salty. You want her, go get her."

"Well, it's not that simple." I slumped against the counter beside him with a sigh. "She's not like that."

"Like what?"

I shrugged, searching for the words, completely aware what my admission meant. Sarah was well and truly under my skin, and I had no idea how to handle it. "She's not like us. She has a nine-to-five, drives a leased car, and doesn't party." I shrugged again, wishing I knew a better way to say it. "She's a good girl."

A heavy hand landed on my shoulder. "Son, if she's a good girl, then she's worth having."

"Yeah, she is, for the right man. She's not my type, though." Far from it. Sarah was everything clean and decent, not some whore to hook up with for a while until something better came along.

"Who's to say who the right man is?" Badger slapped my back hard enough to nearly knock me over. "You boys, too damn dense to see what's right in front of you. I don't know about you." He refilled his mug from the now full pot, and headed back to the porch, muttering about stupid boys.

Crazy old man had no fucking clue. I poured my coffee and headed back to work. All I needed was a way to fill my time and thoughts until she faded from memory. Simple. Just like anything else I wanted, and couldn't have, I needed to simply move on.

I planted myself in front of my computer and spent the next two hours helping another criminal hide his ill-gotten gains. The little thrill I always took in the work remained conspicuously absent. Nothing satisfied me since I came back from Oklahoma. Nothing except staring at the photo of Sarah on my phone. I spent hours looking at her, daydreaming, remembering. I'd captured her softly smiling, looking sated and happy, just a short time after I'd fucked her senseless.

Yet her carefully worded text waited, unanswered. *"Hi. Just thinking of U, hoping U made it home OK."*

I didn't have the fucking balls to reply. If I did, I might give in to the intense need for her, and beg her to come to me. I couldn't fucking do that. She had a life, a good one. One day, a good man would come along for her, and she would be happy. The only thing I could bring her was destruction. So, in what was likely the only truly decent act of my life, I let her text sit there without a reply.

Yeah, it was a shit thing to do, but I told myself she probably didn't care that much one way or the other. I wasn't normally one to lie to myself, but in this case, I excused it. The thought of Sarah checking her phone, genuinely worried for me, rubbed my conscience raw.

My phone rang, jarring me out of my thoughts. "Yeah, brother."

"Crank? Is that you?" *FUCK!* Sarah.

Fabio was supposed to call and let me know if the

security I set up at the house was enough. "Uh, Sarah. Yeah."
My brain froze up, addled at the sound of her voice.

"I'm...uh...sorry. I hit your number by mistake.
I'll...uh...let you go. Take care." And just like that, the line went
dead.

I just sat there, for what must have been twenty years,
staring at my phone like it grew two heads and bit me. Fucking
idiot. I had just sat there with my mouth open, and let her
think I didn't want to talk to her.

Had she really dialed me by accident?

The phone rang again, snapping me out of my stupor.
This time I had the sense to check before answering. "Sarah?"

"On second thought, there's something I wanted to say
to you. I expected better from you. You didn't even text back to
let me know you made it home alive. I mean, I knew it was just
a one-time thing, no strings." The image of her pissed burned
into my thoughts. Her cheeks would be flushed, chest heaving.

My dick stirred in response. "I'm sorry." The fuck? I
rarely used that word, and never to a chick. "It was a shit thing.
I just figured you were only being polite."

"Polite? After what we did together? What you did to
me? No, polite is hardly what that was." Her voice rose on her
anger.

Yeah, my dick really liked that. I sighed. Time to put an
end to the little fantasy. "Look, Sarah, I'm not—"

"I know you're not interested in anything more from me
than what you already had. Don't worry." The line went dead
again.

Well, fuck. What was I supposed to do with that? The
right thing, the decent thing, would have been to let her stay
mad. Whatever attachment she felt would fade, and she would
go on with her life, the way it was meant to be. Did I ever do

the right thing? Yeah, no.

I tapped out the text. *I want to taste your pussy again.* A long moment passed before I hit send. I waited, but no reply came. Not that I really expected one. She probably hated me. And that was a good thing, for her, at least.

The knock on the door interrupted my vague impulse to send another message. "Yeah?"

Fabio stuck his head in the door. "Got a minute?"

"Yeah, come on in." The distraction would be a good thing. Maybe the impulse to make a fool of myself over some chick would fade in a few minutes. "'Sup?"

"You have any time to dig into that motherfucker at CPS?" Fabio obviously still wanted to bring down the bastard supervisor that sent his niece and nephew to some hellhole foster home for a kickback.

"Not much on him yet. Basic background shit. Barely skated through college, fucking jock. Divorced the former beauty queen to fuck the cute young neighbor. I'm looking for gambling debts, that kind of shit." The quick and dirty rundown made me feel guilty. I should have worked on that shit instead of staring at Sarah's photo with a hard-on.

Fabio nodded. "A'ight, man, just wanted to check. I want to burn that motherfucker to the ground." Rage flashed across his face, gone so quickly only someone who knew him well could have spotted it. "Tyler asked about you. He's wondering when he gets a chance to crush you on that video game again."

Fuck. More guilt heaped up. It wasn't the kid's fault I had my head up my ass over a woman. "If it's okay, I'll come over this evening." I could give up a couple hours of sinking myself into a bottle of whiskey for Tyler.

A quick grin. "Good. See you around seven. Kid will have the game set up and ready for you." The fucker got endless amusement from my inability to keep up with a five year-old in a video game. Different story when I smoked his ass at GTA, though.

After Fabio left, I turned back to work, checking on my inquiries about the CPS supervisor. Nothing yet, but my sources were solid. If there was anything to be found, I would dig it up.

The rumble of my stomach, demanding food, interrupted the coding for a gambling site I owed another club. Time for a break anyway. My legs were cramped from sitting for so long. A good stretch later, I shut everything down and headed for the kitchen. Hopefully, some of the old ladies had brought in something good I could just reheat.

Cherry greeted me with a hug, like always, when I reached the kitchen. The older woman had sort of adopted all the Hell Raiders after her ol' man was killed. And we looked out for her. She was family.

"How you doin', mama?" I hugged her back.

Her genuine smile reached her eyes and lit them. "I'm good, Crank. Really good. But I hear you've been in a foul mood lately."

The shrug I gave even felt unconvincing. "Just been busy. No big deal."

"Bull-fucking-shit. Don't you forget who you talkin' to, son." The look she gave me said very clearly she had no intention of accepting excuses, or letting it drop.

Fine. "Okay, I've fuckin' got a lot on my mind. Nothing for any of the nosy motherfuckers around here to worry about." The hurt in her face kicked me in the gut as I stepped around her to the fridge.

"Crank!" The anger in Badger's tone almost froze me in my tracks.

I spun to meet him as he strode into the kitchen. "The fuck, old man?"

That old fucker got right up in my face. "You know I love you like a son, Crank, but if I ever hear you use such a disrespectful tone to Cherry again, I will fucking end you."

The words gave me pause, for an instant. "Fuck you. I'm sick of every fucking body around here trying to pry into my shit. Ain't none y'all's business what's on my mind." I wanted to say a hell of a lot more, but good sense made me stop while I was ahead.

"You stupid little bastard. The instant you come in here acting like a fucking bull in the breeding pens, growling at everybody that looks at you, breaking shit, and disrespecting people, whatever the fuck you got on that tiny little brain of yours becomes *all* our fucking business. Now quit being a little cocksucker and get your shit squared. I don't give a shit if you go get fucked, get fucked up, or fuck somebody up, you get it squared away." The speech ended abruptly, and he stepped away from me to slip his arms around Cherry.

Well, when the fuck did *that* happen?

I stomped out and headed around the back of the house. It pained me to admit it, but Badger was right. I was letting the way I felt about Sarah interfere with shit. If I wasn't careful, I would let it burn bridges I couldn't afford to have burned. I had to find a way to fucking get her out of my system.

CHAPTER 2

Sarah:

For the tenth time in an hour, I slid my phone back into my pocket. Texting or calling Crank again was futile. He'd had his fun, and now he'd gone back to his life. All his sweet words meant nothing at all. He thought I was beautiful alright, for just exactly as long as it took him to get into my pants. To my shame, he accomplished that in record speed. I'd all but fell right into his bed, despite my usual rule about not sleeping with a man unless we were exclusive, at the very least. I should have known better.

A man like him, used to life on the edge, free to pursue anything that interested him, could never be interested in someone like me beyond the few minutes it took him to add another notch in his belt. He probably got a huge kick out of telling his friends about the boring little girl he spent time with here; the good girl who listened to pop music, drove a hybrid car, and had veggie pizza with a rented DVD every Friday night.

The thought of some sexy, adventurous biker chick under him, with his hands and mouth on her, turned my stomach. Of course, that's what Crank was used to. I was such a fool for falling for his little game, and entertaining him while he had to stay here to help his friend.

I sucked up my hurt feelings yet again, left my phone in

my pocket, and tried to concentrate on the paperwork I needed to finish. In the four weeks since Crank left, my mind tended to wonder, and work I normally found tolerable suddenly bored me to tears.

Mr. Sennit, my supervisor, seemed to be punishing me, too. Probably for my part in his losing whatever kickback he expected for placing the Blair children in the Thomas home long-term. Since then, I suddenly had an influx of new cases, meaning mountains more paperwork, and less time for home visits, or following through with my children.

Terrified of letting something terrible slip through the cracks because I had too many cases, I compensated by coming in early and staying late to take care of the paperwork. The stupid reports had to be done, and the forms all filed, because those provided the concrete evidence of my job performance. Too many caseworkers shortened visits and interviews in order to keep up with the paperwork, and tragedies occurred because of it.

The office phone buzzed, interrupting my wondering thoughts. "Sarah Channing."

"Miss Channing, my office please. I need to discuss a case with you." Mr. Sennit sounded almost gleeful.

My stomach churned with anxiety. "Of course. I'll be right there." Had I let something slip? I searched my memory, looking for some mistake, something I might have let go in my rush to get on to the next case. With a sigh, I pushed back from the desk, and headed for the Supervisor's office.

The walk only served to increase my fear, so by the time I tapped at Mr. Sennit's door, my stomach threatened to empty itself right there on his floor.

"Ah, Miss Channing. Good to see you. Please, close the door and have a seat." Mr. Sennit sat behind his immaculate desk, white shirt enhancing his tanned features. He kept his sleeves turned back to reveal muscular forearms, and several of the women in the office appreciated that a bit more than they should. Lately, heavily tattooed arms interested me far more.

I closed the door softly, and sat on the edge of one of the chairs. "What can I do for you, Mr. Sennit?"

He flashed his handsome smile. "Well, for one, you can call me Jared. Mr. Sennit is my father, and makes me sound ancient."

I nodded, but didn't reply. A devilish grin with a slightly chipped tooth, accented by a hoop through a sexy lower lip, held far more appeal for me than the artificially whitened perfect smile in front of me.

The smile never wavered. "Besides that, I have a couple of things. First, we have a new caseworker, which should help some with the overload. I'd like you to show her the ropes. Helena Stark, fresh out of college, starts tomorrow. I need her to shadow you, for say, a week, then we'll start giving her tasks and see how it goes."

Dread filled me. Training a new person, even if they already knew the job, was time consuming. This one had no clue, and it would be weeks before she would be ready to lighten the burden. "I can do that, of course." It meant I would fall even further behind, and have to work harder and longer to make sure all my cases received the attention they needed. "What else?"

"I'm a little hesitant after the way the Blair case went, but a folder just came to me that involves an old school friend. I promised to put my best on it, both because of the old friendship, and because of the seriousness of the complaint. I'd like you to handle this one." A file dropped to the desk with a little snap that startled me.

I reached for it, even though every instinct warned me to refuse the case. "What is it?"

His smile widened, like the cat who ate the canary. "Julia Garret, and her husband, Matt, are foster parents. Three children are placed with them. The eldest, a twelve-year-old female, went to the school nurse complaining of painful urination. After a brief interview, the girl asserted that Mr. Garret touched her inappropriately. The nurse immediately stopped the interview, brought in the school counselor, and called me."

"And you want me to investigate the claims? Why?" Confusion buzzed through my mind. What sort of traps might he have waiting within this case?

"I do. Because you're my best caseworker at the moment, and because you seem to have an intuitive ability to sense when things aren't right, like with the Blair children." He grinned, his attempt at flirting coming far short of the mark. "Will you do it?"

I shrugged, uncomfortable. "Why are you even asking? Normally you would just assign me the case."

His face turned serious, concerned. "Because I need your assurance that you'll give this case the attention it deserves. Any allegation of mistreatment within a foster home is very serious, of course, but this one, because of the nature of the allegation, is vital. The Garrets, of course, will be greatly impacted if the allegations are founded, but either outcome will impact this office."

I sighed inwardly. So this was what it felt like when your boss had it out for you and decided you needed to self-destruct. "I'll handle it carefully, of course, but given the number of cases I already have, I'm not certain why you're giving it to me. Surely someone else, even you, could give it more attention?"

The anger crossed his face so quickly I almost missed it. "I have to be strictly hands off, because of the personal connection. I might be able to shift a couple of your cases to others, but everyone is overloaded at the moment."

I suppressed a shiver and nodded. "Of course. I'll do my best." I stood, bade him a good afternoon, and left. Every self-defense mechanism I possessed shrieked with the alarm. Jared Sennit was not a man I wanted angry at me.

As I passed Melissa Tate's office, she called out to me. "Hey, Sarah, you got a sec?"

I smiled. What trouble had my best friend cooked up this time? Inside her office, I closed the door. "What's up, Mel?"

"First, we need a girls night. I've been waiting patiently, but you still haven't dished about the hot biker." Ice rattled in the takeout cup as she took a sip of whatever drink she'd brought back from lunch.

"I'm sorry, Mel. All these new cases are stretching me to the limit, and now Mr. Sennit just gave me another one, a huge one." Guilt assaulted me. Mel was always there for me, without fail, even when it wasn't convenient for her. I owed her the same courtesy.

"Stop frowning, goofball. You're too serious. And what do you mean by new cases? I haven't had anything new hit my desk in two weeks. I was starting to wonder if everyone suddenly started being good to their kids."

"What?" I tried to contain my temper as her words sank in. "Are you serious? Nothing new in two weeks?"

My seriousness penetrated her joking demeanor. "Let me double check, but at least two weeks." She flipped through her planner. "Seventeen days since my last new case."

"Ughhh! That bastard!" The anger slipped a little.

"Who? What happened?" Concern furrowed her brow.

A deep breath did nothing to calm me. "Mel, I've had *seven* new cases in that same amount of time."

Her perfectly made up eyes widened dramatically. "Oh, shit! What's going on? Why is he doing that?"

Tension bit into my shoulders. "I don't know." I had my suspicions, though. I stood. "Look, I need to get on this new one right away. Can I stop by when I finish for the night? I'll bring wine."

Mel came from behind her desk and folded me into a warm hug. "Sweetie, you can come over any time, even if you forget the wine."

I returned the hug, promised to call, and headed back to my office to review the file on the Garret case. It seemed straight-forward, but with sexual abuse allegations, nothing was ever simple. The details absorbed me quickly, and I gathered my things to go make initial contact.

A short time later, I sat in a cramped resource room at the middle school with the eerily pretty girl, and the school counselor. The interview left no doubt in my mind that the Garret house needed further investigation. The things the little girl described happening to her absolutely turned my stomach. I met the counselor's horrified gaze, and gave a warning shake of my head. Any indication of shock or dismay from us, and the girl might shut down.

I finished with my notes. "Remy, I want you to understand exactly how serious this is, and what will happen next. There are going to be tons of questions, some of them embarrassing, and there'll be a doctor, and a psychologist, probably lawyers, and maybe even court. It isn't going to be fun, either for you, or Mr. Garret. If there's anything you want to change about what you said, now is the time." I waited while she absorbed my words.

"You think I'm lying?" Her lip trembled.

"I just want to be sure I have all the details right, sweetie, nothing more." I actually believed her. She knew more about sex than any twelve-year-old should, and not things that could be gleaned from porn or romance novels. A girl her age could, of course, be sexually active, but the things she described weren't consistent with a fumbling teenage boy. "Have you talked to anyone at all about this before?"

"I tried to tell Mr. Sennit, my regular caseworker." The words fell like bricks, and the counselor met my gaze, fully aware of the implications.

"What did he say?"

Remy shrugged. "He laughed a little, and said I had a vivid imagination." Her gaze dropped and she worried at her lip with her teeth. "Then he said maybe I could suck his cock for him."

My heart leapt into my throat. If what this girl said was true, my boss could be a pedophile, along with being a crook. A sick feeling settled into my stomach. How many other girls had he propositioned? Had he actually assaulted any of them?

Did he think I wouldn't find out? Surely he couldn't be so arrogant as to think the girl would stay silent? Yes. Yes, he could. Jared Sennit was the personification of arrogance and conceit.

Slowly, the magnitude of what lay ahead sank into my brain. If I took this one allegation to the district supervisor, especially before I completed my investigation, I risked giving myself a reputation of being eager to get a coworker into trouble. It was hardly unheard of for a juvenile in the system to make such accusations because of some perceived slight, or just because they felt like making trouble. No, I had to proceed carefully.

I finished up the interview, gathered my notes, and left to make arrangements for Remy to be placed in a group home until the investigation could be finished. Either way, she wouldn't return to the Garret home.

Nausea built as I drove back to the office. I kept trying to focus on the task ahead, make a mental roadmap of the steps I needed to take. By the time I parked the car, I barely made it out of my seat in time to empty my stomach on the pavement.

CHAPTER 3

Crank:

The fucking wood cracked under the force of my blow. God damn it. Something, besides the fucking practice dummy, had to give soon. Almost five weeks. It had been almost five weeks since I left Sarah, and instead of fading, this irrational need for her kept growing. Every fucking moment turned into a battle not to get on my bike and get back to her as fast as I could go. I had to constantly remind myself I could bring her nothing good. I destroyed shit. Everything I fucking touched turned to shit. I refused to do that to her life.

I gave the practice dummy one last vicious kick, and stepped back, breathing hard, dripping sweat. What the fuck was wrong with me? I had never dealt with this kind of distraction before. I could always clear my head for work, or training, but now, every thought came with a reminder of Sarah.

I tried drinking it away, and Mr. Jack Daniels became my best friend for a minute, but even he failed to drown the need. Fucking other women turned out to be laughable. Sure, I did it, and I got off, but only by fantasizing about Sarah. The stupor of pills made it worse, carrying my mind directly to her. I seriously contemplated the oblivion H could give me, but I knew even that relief would only be temporary, and would leave me chasing it. The Hell Raiders weren't nice boys, and we all did a lot of shit, but serious drugs were where Kellen drew the line. Especially since all the bullshit Hack put us through.

Kellen came in through the open wall of the old shed we had converted into a makeshift gym. "Damn, Brother, you been working hard." He took in the busted dummy. "Remind me to stay the fuck out of your way."

I threw a dirty look his way. "What of it?" Fucking sweat dripped into my eyes.

"Nothing at all, man." He raised his hands at his sides, as if in surrender. "You see yourself in the mirror lately?"

"Now why the fuck would I do that?"

"Motherfucker, you've lost weight. You've been out here so much you're even more ripped than usual. And you look like the hounds of hell are hot on your tail." He shook his head. "You need a break, man. Or something."

The glare I sent his way must have been scary as fuck, because Kellen took a half step back. "Yeah. Or something. All the fuck I need is for all the motherfuckers around here to quit digging in my shit."

"Fair enough. Not digging in your shit. But I am telling you, get that shit straight. You're no good to me if you work yourself into a stupor." He flipped me off and headed back toward the clubhouse.

"Fuck you, too, cocksucker." I turned back to the mess I'd made of the sparring dummy. I couldn't very well beat the hell out of it anymore, so I needed to clean the shit up and see about fixing it. Maybe that would occupy a little more time. Keep my head out of my ass a few minutes.

An hour later, I made my way back inside, exhausted and starved. A shower might help, but I didn't even have the energy left for that shit. Instead, I went straight to my room and fell into bed. Fuck it. No one cared if I stunk to high fucking heaven or not.

Darkness sucked me under, and I must have slept for a long fucking time. An annoying buzz kept tugging at me, pulling me back to the surface. When I opened my eyes, the only light came from the bluish glow around the edge of my phone where it lay screen-down on my pillow.

I rolled over with a groan and rubbed the sleep out of my eyes. The goddamn phone started buzzing again and I snatched it up, intent on cussing someone the fuck out.

"Sarah", the screen said.

"Sarah? Is that you?" My heart jumped into my throat as I answered. Could she really be calling me? After all this time?

"Crank? I'm sorry to bother you. I just didn't know where else to turn." Her voice trembled. Fear? Why would she be that fucking scared?

"What's wrong, Sarah?" Blood rushed through my veins, pounded in my head, driving me to get to her, protect her.

"I...I got information on my boss, the one that sent Tyler and Nicole—"

"I remember. What's wrong?" If I sounded harsh, I didn't mean to, but I needed to know what the fuck was wrong, and right away.

"It's worse than kickbacks, Crank. So far, I've found three girls he's raped."

Silence pounded between us. "Sarah, does he know you found out?" Fuck.

"I...I think so." She took a deep breath, obviously gathering her courage. "I came home from work, and my apartment had been broken into. Some notes I made were missing."

FuckfuckFUCK. "Where are you now? Are you alone?"

"I'm in my car now, alone. I don't feel safe in my apartment, and I really don't have anywhere to go." She sounded small, and terrified.

"Okay, baby. I want you to drive to the next town, and a get a hotel room. Call off sick, and wait for me there. Order in, don't go out for anything. Understood?" The plan came together in my head like loading my weapons. Quick and easy. I was already on my feet, throwing my shit into a bag.

"I could go to my friend's house—"

"You could. If you want to bring this cocksucker after your friend, too. A hotel is better, keeps other people out of the line of fire." Shit, she just wanted someone with her, and I couldn't blame her for that. "Maybe have your friend come and meet you there?" I hated that thought, since it gave the asshole another opportunity to find her, but if waiting alone in a hotel bothered her that much, it was worth the risk.

She stayed silent for a moment. "Okay, I think I have someone who could do that."

"Good. You called the cops? Got everything secured?" As much as I despised the idea of cops being involved, in this case, it seemed necessary.

"Yes. The officers came, went through the apartment with me, and advised me to spend the night somewhere else. They stayed while I packed a bag and helped me lock up." She sounded a little stronger. The presence of the cops reassured her a little. Good to know.

"Okay, then, start driving. Stay in busy areas, in as much traffic as possible. It's not easy at night, but pay attention to the cars around you. If you see the same one more than a couple times, you need to change routes quickly." My hands shook with the need to take care of her, to keep this cocksucker from hurting her any further.

"Alright." A short pause. "Crank?"

"Yeah?"

"Thank you. I knew you would take me seriously, even if we didn't end things on a great note."

I stayed silent for a moment. "Baby, I don't consider us ended." *Shut the fuck up, motherfucker.* "I'll be there as soon as I can get there. You fucking stay safe. Understood?"

"Okay." She sounded small and quiet and scared, and my fucking arms ached to hold her.

I ended the call and hurried to throw the rest of my shit in the bag, then headed out to find Kellen. Motherfucker was nowhere to be found, so I settled for Trip. I gave a quick explanation of the call from Sarah, and said I had to go, and I'd be in touch. At the same time, I was on my phone, booking a flight. As much as I preferred to have my bike, and my hardware, I refused to take that much time getting to her. I would pick up whatever I needed when I got there.

"You need backup?" The fucking concern in Trip's voice made me impatient.

The urge to roll my eyes like a teenager hit hard, but I resisted. "I'll call if I run into trouble, or reach out to some of the people we know close by. Ain't tryin' to do anything stupid."

"A'ight, man, go take care of your woman. While you're at it, get your shit together."

"Yeah, yeah." I flipped him off and headed for the door.

The drive to the airport stretched on forever, and GPS made my life easier as I navigated the maze of lanes that led every-damn-where. I parked the car in the short-term parking, gathered my shit, and headed inside. Getting through security turned into a nightmare. People in the long line gave me a wide berth, but they still grated on my nerves. Then the TSA dude made me empty my pockets, take off my boots, and still fucking patted me down.

An hour and a half after I left the car, I sat my hillbilly ass in the secure area of the airport, and waited for my flight to be called. Apparently, people watching was not an acceptable pastime for big, rough-looking tattooed bikers. At least, I gathered that from the reactions of everyone who happened to notice me watching them. Before long, people actively avoided my section of seats, which suited me just fine.

Finally, my flight boarded. I found my seat, stowed my shit in the overhead compartment, and took my seat. At least I got a window seat. Seconds after I said my thanks for that piece of good luck, a harried-looking woman in an airline uniform practically shoved a kid into the seat next to me.

"This is where you stay until I come get you." She leaned in and buckled his seat belt. "Do not get up, and do not bother anyone. Do you understand?"

The kid, who I guessed to be about ten, grinned and nodded. The woman rolled her eyes and rushed away. The kid looked at me. "Are those tattoos real?"

I glared back. "Why the hell wouldn't they be? Of course they are."

He shrugged, all dramatic like. "I don't know. You could be some pussy wanna-be with the kind that washes off."

A bark of laughter escaped me before I could stop it. "Your momma let you say shit like that?"

"Don't have one anymore, so I can say whatever I want."

I had no reply for that one. Silence suited me better, anyway. The crew made all their announcements, and we started to move. The armrests nearly came off in my hands as the ground dropped away beneath the plane, but once it made cruising altitude, I relaxed.

The kid had no intentions of letting me sleep my way to Oklahoma, though. "So, are you in a biker gang, or what?"

I opened one eye and studied him. "No. I'm a Hell Raider. What are you? Some kind of juvenile delinquent?"

He tilted his head at me. "How did you know?"

"Know what?"

"That I'm a juvenile delinquent."

Fuck. "I didn't. I was just jerking your chain because you asked me about a biker gang. What makes you think you're a juvenile delinquent?" Fuck. The last thing I needed was to know this kid's story. He probably did something stupid and got labeled bad. Sorta like me.

He shrugged again. "My mom said so. Teachers did, too. She doesn't want me anymore, so she sent me to some place that's supposed to make me good. After that, I don't know where I'll live."

Anger rolled over me. "What the fuck you do for them to say that?"

"There was this kid. He always picked on me, but everyone believed him when he said I started it. I tried to stay away from him, but he always hunted for me. One day, he was going to hurt me, like really bad. I hit him in the head with a rock and made him stop." Tears glazed his eyes, but he held them back. "I made him like a vegetable, or something, and I'm not sorry. He deserved it."

"Shit, kid, I'm sorry." Despite myself, I couldn't help feeling sympathy for the kid. He wasn't the first to defend himself and be accused of being the instigator. Hopefully, shit would work out for him.

CHAPTER 4

Sarah:

I sat there in my car, staring at my phone, unable to believe I actually gave in and called Crank. I probably should have a couple weeks ago, when I found out Sennit raped girls he was supposed to protect. The very thought still sent a vortex of anger whirling through me. From his reaction, I was pretty sure Crank felt the same way.

I don't know why I even called him. I just didn't know anyone else who might be able to help me, now that Sennit probably knew for sure that I had been looking into his cases. The police and prosecutors were the obvious answers, of course, but Sennit had standing poker games with several men connected high up with both. My family and friends could be hurt, if they even believed me. Crank owed me nothing, but at least he seemed to take me seriously. That was more than I'd really expected. And he was hardly the kind of man who ran scared from a pedophile, no matter how well connected.

From our short acquaintance, I knew Crank had a gentle side, and felt sure he was a good man, in spite of the bad he was capable of doing, and I had no doubt he could do some very bad things. Exactly the kind of man capable of protecting me from Sennit and whoever helped him by breaking into my apartment.

I'd met some of Crank's friends, others in his motorcycle club, and they scared me to death at first. But I quickly learned they were simply a large family. A loud, boisterous family with quirks, but they loved each other. What was it like to belong to something like that?

As overwhelming as I found them at first, I couldn't help but envy the women those Hell Raiders claimed as their own. Their men left no doubt they would do absolutely anything to protect them. I couldn't imagine having a man look at me like the one called Trip looked at Tanya. He would kill for her, maybe already had. I had never seen that kind of devotion in real life before.

I wrenched my mind back to the present. Where could I go? He said another town. Okay, then. I put the car in Drive, glad I'd fueled up when I got off work. I drove through the night, in a near-panic, searching my mirrors for any car I'd seen before. As the miles passed, I started to settle down and not worry quite so much.

I ended up taking a roundabout route, and after nearly an hour, finally pulled into the lot of a small hotel. Maybe this was all unnecessary. Some of it might even be my imagination. I should just go back to my apartment, clean up the shambles the burglar left, and go to work in the morning, like always. If I acted completely normal—

My phone buzzed with an incoming text from an unknown number. *"2nite wuz a prevu. Stop."*

My heart pounded in my chest. Suddenly, I was very clear on things. It didn't matter if I did over react. Sennit hurt those girls. And he had no intention of facing charges for that, at the very least. Any man capable of raping teen girls, and calling it a deal to be sure they remained in a good placement, would stop at nothing, including murder, to hide his activities. That text served as a convenient little reminder, and I was grateful. Without it, I might have made a deadly mistake.

I gathered up my courage, along with my bags, locked my car carefully, and went inside to get a room. The bored clerk didn't give me a second glance before sliding two keycards across the counter to me. I hoped he paid a little more attention if anyone came around asking questions about the guests here. With my luck, he would just slide another keycard over to them.

The carpeting in the lobby showed a little wear, but seemed clean, and I found the same in the corridor when I stepped off the elevator. When I found my room, all the way at the end of the hall, I fumbled with the keycard for a minute, then finally the light on the lock turned green and let me in.

The light came on in the little entryway when I flicked the switch, and I dragged my stuff inside and closed the door behind me. The room turned out to be nicer than I expected, with a big soft bed, fluffy pillows, and thick towels in the spotless bathroom. The walls were papered in what looked to be a reproduction vintage paper, and the bedding matched.

The closet had plenty of space for the few things I brought along. Maybe tomorrow I could stop back by my apartment and pick up some clothes, at least. If this turned into anything longer than a couple days, I would definitely need to.

My phone buzzed as I kicked my shoes off and settled on the side of the bed. Crank's number this time. *"You safe, baby?"*

I smiled and tapped out my reply. *"Yes, thx. At hotel now."* When he asked, I gave him the specifics, and he said he had to go, but he would see me soon.

I felt unaccountably safe in that knowledge. Crank was the kind of man I would normally avoid at all costs. Rough. My mother would call him a hoodlum, with his tattoos, worn jeans, and leather, not to mention the motorcycle. The pierced lip would be the final straw for her.

A chill raced over my skin. Shit. My mother! I needed to let my parents, and a couple of close friends know what happened, and that I wasn't home. Oh, God, what if my mom stopped by to drop something off, as she often did, and saw the after-effects of the burglary? She would be terrified.

I hurried to dial, so I could make sure she didn't accidentally endanger herself. "Mom, hi—"

"Oh, hi, Sarah. I can't believe you didn't tell me about this young man." Anticipation practically gushed from her voice.

Confusion slowed my thoughts, and dread settled into my stomach. "Which young man, Mom?"

She laughed. "The one you work with, silly girl. He says you've been seeing each other for the last few months, but had to keep it secret."

Oh. My. God. My stomach heaved and I dropped the phone in my mad dash for the toilet. Sennit was *there*, at my parents' house, telling them all sorts of lies to cover his tracks. And the threat was crystal clear. Say the wrong thing, and they could suffer harm. Simple.

Finally, I composed myself, and found my phone. The call had ended, presumably when I didn't respond. I hurried to dial again. "Sorry, Mom, I think I ate something bad."

"Oh, thank goodness, sweetie. I was worried. So when were you going to tell us about him?" Mom had hounded me since I finished college to find 'a nice young man' and give her grandchildren, and now she thought I had the first part of the job completed.

"Is he still there, Mom?" I held my breath.

"No, I'm sorry, sweetie, he had to leave. A call came in about an abused child." She continued to chatter, oblivious.

I tried to think fast. How could I make sure my parents stayed safe and beyond Sennit's reach? I interrupted her. "Mom, you know that cruise you and dad always wanted to take?"

She laughed. "Of course. Don't tell me you're planning a wedding on a cruise ship! That would be just too romantic."

I tried to laugh it off. "No, Mom, nothing like that. Something I invested in a while back has paid off. I want you and Dad to pack for a cruise, and go to the airport by noon. Everything you need will be waiting at the Information kiosk. Just do me a favor, and don't tell anyone until after you leave. I'd rather avoid awkward questions about my investments, you know?" I prayed silently that she would accept the story and agree. The stroke of inspiration seemed too good, even if it meant maxing out my credit cards.

"Sarah, don't joke about things like this. You know your father's heart—"

"I'm not joking, Mom. I don't know the details yet, but by noon, I'll have the two of you booked for the cruise of your dreams." *Please don't argue with me.* I had no clue how long it took to book a nice cruise, or even how much it really cost, but I was about to find out. "Now, do as I ask, and lock everything up tight, get a good night's rest, and pack in the morning. And remember, don't tell anyone yet."

The long pause made me think she hung up on me. "Are you sure, Sarah?"

"I've never been more sure of anything, Mom. I want to do this for you."

She laughed a little. "In that case, I'll see you tomorrow. We'll stop by your place for a hug before we go to the airport."

"NO!" What was I supposed to tell her now? There was a reason I was always a good kid. I couldn't lie to save my life.

"Uh, you can't. I'm not there."

"Oh? Where are you?"

Now what? "I, uh, ran into an old friend today, so we're catching up. Since it's so late, I'm just going to get a room for the night, and go straight to work in the morning." I prayed that made some sort of sense.

"Oh, a girl friend?" Leave it to my mom's suspicious nature to kick in now, instead of when Sennit sat at her table and told her he and I were secretly involved.

"Yes, from college." Any guilt I might have felt for lying quickly disappeared under the need to keep my parents safe. Sennit had my apartment broken into, and had me threatened. Until he gave it up, I had no idea which line he would refuse to cross. At this point, I suspected there wasn't one. "She lived on my floor in the dorm senior year, and I haven't heard from her in a long time."

"Oh. Okay, then. I guess we'll save the hugs for when we get back."

I nearly collapsed with relief. "Good. Now, go lock up, and get some rest. You're going to need it." We said our goodnights, and Mom promised to call before they left for the airport.

When I ended the call, I threw myself back onto the bed, breathing hard, as if I'd run a marathon or something. My pulse finally settled back into something like the normal range, and I quickly called Melissa.

She answered with her usual enthusiasm and affection. "The hell, bitch?"

I laughed. "Just wanted to let you know, I have to be out of town for a few days, so I won't be at work." Getting something past her would be far more difficult than lying to my mother.

"Oh? You find another hot biker to fuck?" She never failed to remind me of the time I spent with Crank, but it worked in my favor this time.

I laughed. "Not another one."

"You're kidding! Sarah, that bastard left you, high and dry. Why are you wasting more time on him?" Her inner bitch came out fighting.

"It wasn't like that, and you know it. He's not relationship material, but that doesn't mean he's not fun." I almost believed myself with that one.

"Well, when you put it like that...Okay, tell me everything." I could practically see her grin.

I debated how much to tell her. "Well, I've been in contact a couple of times since he left here." She didn't know about the text, or the phone call. I'd been too humiliated to share that part. "I talked to him today, and we arranged to meet."

My best friend's squee of excitement split my eardrum. "Oh, my God! That's so...HOT!"

"Don't get carried away, goofy. It's no big deal."

"Bullshit. I saw the way you looked after you were with him. That man moves the earth for you. So if there's any possibility, you had better grab on with both hands." She talked on, about predestined soul mates, and fate, and a bunch of other things, no doubt, gleaned from the books she read.

I humored her, and listened, all while cautioning myself not to read anything into what Crank said about us not being ended. Finally, she wound down, and I said goodnight, after promising to give her all the juicy details later. Was it a bad thing that I found myself hoping there *were* juicy details?

CHAPTER 5

Crank:

By the time we landed, I knew a fuck-ton more about the kid than I wanted, and none of it made me happy. But that wasn't my battle, and there wasn't a fucking thing I could do about it, other than give him a little advice.

"Li'l man, you might have to do what the grown-ups tell you right now, fucked up as it is, but one day you'll be on your own. Then, if you want to be a real man, you own your shit, and you take care of what's yours. Family ain't always blood, and when you find yours, you hold them close, and never let go. Got me?" Hell, it was probably above his head, but he might find it useful in the future.

"Got you." When the harried looking woman came to get him, he gave me a solemn salute, and followed her without complaint.

Finally, I grabbed my shit and got off the damn plane. If I never flew again, it would be too fucking soon. Thankfully, I called ahead for a car, and the rental place had an SUV waiting for me. I hated cars, but at least I didn't have to ride in a beer can rolling down the road. The GPS fucked around at first, but after a couple of tries, I got the details for Sarah's hotel plugged in, and the thing brought up the directions.

The drive took forever, or felt like it, but finally, I parked the rented SUV outside the hotel just after four a.m., and dragged my tired ass inside. Knocking on Sarah's door in the middle of the night seemed like a bad idea, so I paused just inside the lobby to call her and let her know I was coming up.

"Sir? Excuse me, can I help you?" The pudgy clerk in too-tight khakis and polo hurried my way. If the boy didn't slow down, he was going to lose his coke-bottle glasses.

"I'm good. Just calling my girl to let her know I'm here." I turned away a little to dial Sarah.

"Uh, Sir? I can't allow you to disturb our guests." He stroked the patchy scruff on his face, as if seeking comfort from it.

I took a deep breath, striving for patience. "Look, man, I'm not disturbing any fucking guests. I'm calling my girl before I go up, so I don't startle her."

Fucker gave a long-suffering sigh. "Sir, I'm sorry. Our guests pay a premium for privacy." He sounded like someone trying to explain a simple concept to a stubborn child. "So, you see, I can't have anyone loitering in the lobby to make a phone call."

Enough. "Listen, you measly little cocksucker. I've had a very long fucking day, so I'm only saying this one time. Your guest in room three-twelve is waiting for me. Now, I'm going to call her, and let her know I'm here, and coming up. And you are going to go back to the desk, and mind your own fucking business. Understand?"

He paled, but nodded, and followed orders. Thank fuck. I'd hate to mess up the damn lobby of the hotel.

With the bastard out of my hair, I took my time and dialed Sarah. She answered quickly. "You safe, baby?"

"Mmm, Crank. Yes, I am. I think I actually went to sleep, too." Her drowsy voice did all kinds of things to me, but I refused to think about that for the moment.

I headed for the elevators. "Well, how about you drag

that delicious little ass out of bed and open the door for me?"

"Open—Wait, you're here?"

"Three-twelve, right?" The elevator dinged as it started upward.

"Right. Oh my God, I can't believe you're already here." Her phone jostled around as she moved. "I thought it would be a couple of days, at least."

The elevator stopped with another ding, and the doors rattled open. I stepped out, and there she was, three doors down on the left. She looked so fucking delicious in her little nightshirt and shorts, with all that blonde hair tousled around her shoulders, and her face flushed a little from sleep. My dick gave an immediate twitch of approval.

I stopped, right there in the hall, and just soaked in the sight of her. A knot of tension I hadn't even known existed began to unfurl in my gut. Seeing Sarah again...it just felt right. The distance between us closed and I swept her into my arms. Gathering her warm, soft body to mine felt like coming home, and I never wanted to fucking leave that moment.

Long before I finished breathing her in, she drew back a little. "We should, uh...go inside." She made a vague gesture toward the open door behind her.

"Yeah, we probably should." Taking my hands off her seemed like sacrilege, so I allowed her to guide me into her room while I maintained my hold on her. The moment I passed the threshold, I kicked the door shut as we continued on into the room. "You were sleeping. I'm sorry for waking you."

White teeth sank into her full lower lip for an instant before she spoke. "I'm not. I'm glad you're here." She stared up at me for a moment. "And not just because I'm scared to death."

My heart thudded hard in my chest. She was glad to see

me. Fuck, I needed to put that aside, and just deal with making sure she stayed safe. "I should have called you before."

She smiled a little and pressed close to me again. "Yes, you should have." She slid her hands up my chest and around the back of my neck, then stood on her tiptoes and reached up to brush her lips over mine.

Any good intentions in me went right out the window. Maybe I couldn't protect her from myself, but I would damn sure make sure no one else harmed her. The strap slipped from my shoulder and my heavy bag hit the floor with a thud. I didn't give a fuck.

I leaned into her and absolutely possessed her mouth, nipping and probing until she opened for me, then sweeping in to caress the tender flesh she offered. Her willingness made my dick surge with heat for her, and tore a long groan from me. I pulled her closer, molding her body to mine.

Sarah moaned and wrapped her legs around my waist as I lifted her. Only a few strides carried us to the bed, and I let her slide down to the mattress. The thin nightshirt came easily over her head, and she raised her arms to let me remove it completely. I had to stop and look at her in the low light from the entryway.

Pale golden skin glowed, begging my touch. She looked up at me, lips parted, beautiful tits rising and falling with every breath. My hands ached to be filled with her flesh, but I waited. I bent and hooked my fingers in the waist of her little shorts and pulled them off. The lacy white panties went next. She lifted her ass a little to help, and I slid the thin fabric down her long legs.

Sarah laid back, and her hair spilled around her shoulders. She was the most fucking beautiful sight in the world. The need to have her totally consumed me, and I dropped to the edge of the bed to take her mouth again. Her fingers wound in my hair, and her little whimpers drove me to more. Before long, I followed the need and left her mouth, kissing and licking down her neck, along her collar bone, to the valley between her perfect tits, and then to her nipples.

She arched and held me closer as I teased first one hardened peak, then the other. All the sounds she made stoked the fire in my blood and made me want her even more, if that were possible. My hard-on pressed against my jeans, eager for freedom and her sweet heat, forcing me to adjust myself.

I slid further down and gently pressed her legs apart, revealing her to me. Unable to wait and appreciate the view, I moved in to taste her. A groan from the depths of my soul escaped. How the fuck had I lived without this? A little voice in the back of my mind asked how I would go back to living without it again.

I ignored the questions, and turned my full attention to utterly consuming Sarah. Desperate to have her, I fumbled my jeans open and freed my hard-on, with her cries spurring me on.

Fffuucccckkkkk! No condom! As much as I was dying to have her, I couldn't bring myself to do her raw. I hadn't exactly always been safe, and I refused to take that risk with her.

So I spread her further, ate her like a starving man at a buffet, and made her come until she writhed on the bed and begged me to stop. Drawing back, I surveyed my work with satisfaction. Fuck, I could do that every single day, and never come myself, and it would be enough, just to see her have that much pleasure.

She caught her breath, and tugged at my arms, trying to pull me over her.

"Can't, baby. I don't have any condoms right now." God,

it killed me to say that. Any other chick, and I'd have gone right the fuck ahead.

Sarah looked up at me, pleading, needing more. "It's okay. I'm on the pill."

How the fuck was I supposed to tell her something like this? "No, it's not okay. I can't be sure I'm clean, and I won't put you in danger, no matter how much I'm dying to have you right now."

The bed creaked a little as she rose onto her elbow. "Thank you for caring that much." She leaned in to kiss me, and just like that, I was lost all over again.

Small hands pressed against my chest, and I didn't resist, letting her push me onto my back. Goosebumps broke across my belly as she lifted the hem of my shirt. "Sarah..." I couldn't say the words.

"Shh. Stop worrying." She leaned down and brushed damp lips over my ribs.

Beyond any ability to reason, I dragged my shirt off, and when I would have flipped her under me, she took my hands in hers. I froze, waiting to see what she would do. No matter how fucking much I wanted her, I couldn't force her.

Sheets rustled as she moved, but disbelief kept me still. She rose from the bed, then stopped long enough to pull my boots off. Strong tugs slid my jeans down and off, change and keys jingling in my pockets. Sarah pushed between my ankles and climbed on the bed.

My vision swam as she settled onto her knees and leaned down to take me into her mouth. I was already too fucking far gone, so I threaded my fingers through her hair, and let her magic take over. I barely managed to pull her away before I came. About the time my lungs stopped heaving for air, I wrapped her into my arms and pulled her close.

"I'm glad you're here." She relaxed against my chest.

"Yeah, me too. I don't know what took me so fucking long to get my ass back here." The admission came unexpectedly. I took a deep breath as I realized it was true. I should have come back to her long ago, or never even fucking left.

The way she rested her head on my chest felt like the most natural thing in the world. "I almost called you, dozens of times every day, to ask you to come back for me."

Fuck. I wished she had. The issues with her boss had to wait until tomorrow. For the moment, I wanted nothing more than to hold my sweet Sarah in my arms and sleep with her. I shifted away from her. "Hang on a second, let me get rid of the rest of these fucking clothes. I don't want anything between us while we sleep." I kicked off my boxer briefs and dropped them on my jeans, along with my socks. I should at least grab the little .22 semi-automatic I picked up on the way from the airport, and keep it handy, but at the moment, I didn't give a fuck. The only thing that mattered was getting back in that bed with Sarah, and just soaking her up.

It only took us a moment to get settled, and although desire for her still burned through my veins, I held off. Right now, she needed comfort more than sex, even mind-blowing sex. And I needed her safe from whatever nastiness might be flowing through my veins. So I pulled her in close, so her hair tickled my jaw, and traced my fingers up and down her spine. The texture of her skin felt like some exotic silk, or some impossibly fine weave of fabric. I could stroke her forever and never tire of it.

Sarah drifted off to sleep, but I lay awake for what seemed a long time. Having her in my arms again felt like some vital part of my body had returned after a long absence. Fuck me, what the hell was I going to do when it was time to go home?

That question brought me right back to the same one I had wrestled with for weeks. Could I ask her to come back to Stags Leap with me? Not really, since she had a life here. But now that trouble seemed to be breathing down her neck with her job, would all that change? If her boss was the sort of low, dirty bastard I figured him for, she would never be safe again while he walked free. Especially not in the same town.

So would she consider relocating for that reason? Or maybe I could talk to Kellen and see about patching to one of the clubs in this area, so I could be close enough to protect her. I could work from anywhere, as long as I had an internet connection. But could I really leave my Brothers, my heritage, and what was left of my family? For a woman?

I wished I knew the answer to that one. My first reaction, the one from my gut, was *Fuck yeah, for Sarah, I could.* But then logic took over, and I just couldn't be so sure.

CHAPTER 6

Sarah:

The sensation of an extremely full bladder woke me. As I started to roll from the bed, I realized I wasn't alone. A strong arm tightened around me when I moved a little. Crank.

He really came for me. A lump formed in my throat. Part of me couldn't believe he actually came. Yes, he'd said to just text or call if I needed him, but people said stuff like that all the time. Especially after he ignored my text at first, and the way I spoke to him when I called that day I was so upset and disappointed. I'd barely allowed myself to hope he might help from a distance. I couldn't blame him if he told me to get lost.

I wriggled away, careful not to wake him, and padded quietly to the bathroom. When I returned and climbed back into the bed, he opened his arms for me to slip back into them. Was he awake? Or just accustomed to having a woman in his bed?

An unexpected spear of jealously hit the vicinity of my heart. I should know better. Crank was hardly the kind of man to settle down to one woman. The way he looked alone would have women crawling all over him, even without that bad boy edge. He probably never slept alone. Tension knotted my muscles and stiffened my body. I didn't want to be just another in a long line of conquests, even though it was too late for that.

"What's wrong, Sarah?" The sleepy rumble of his voice made my stomach do somersaults.

"Nothing. I'm sorry to wake you."

"Bull-fucking-shit. Your stiff as a board. What is it?" He no longer sounded sleepy at all.

I couldn't let him know what I'd been thinking. "Really, nothing is wrong."

He raised onto his elbow and looked down at me. "Do you regret what we did?"

Nothing could be further from the truth. "No, I don't. I'm glad." God, I was a coward. I should just tell him, let him laugh at me and tell me to suck it up. I took a deep breath for courage. "Crank, I'm sorry. I just don't want to be another notch on your belt, and I let myself become exactly that." I started to roll away. He wouldn't want anything more to do with me now. Men like him always ran at the first sign of a woman getting attached.

He pulled me back. "Is that what you think, Sarah? That you're just another fuck to me?" The dim light coming in from the bathroom revealed his frown. "Because I don't know what you did to me, but I haven't been able to get you out of my head since I went back home. All I've been able to do is stare at your picture and dream of you. So, no, you're not another fucking notch on my fucking belt."

His words made my pulse race. Could it be true? Could he actually feel the same attraction, the same need? No, of course not. He probably told all the girls he was with something along the same lines. I searched his face, looking for some hint, anything to tell me if he were sincere.

His lips found my forehead. "Rest for now, Sarah. Tomorrow, we start bringing your boss down. And when that's taken care of, we'll figure this shit between us out. Even though I should get back home as fast as I can, save you the trouble of all the baggage I bring with me, I don't think I can go back without you."

When I started to reply, he shushed me and cradled me close to his chest. The words replayed over and over in my head, long after his breathing evened out with sleep. Did he really mean it? Finally, I dozed off, only to dream of a life far different from the one I led now. One that included Crank.

***

I woke to the sound of my alarm buzzing, and automatically reached to hit snooze. As I snuggled deeper into the bed, memory hit and I scooted over, seeking Crank. He wasn't there. Afraid of the worst, I sat up and wiped the sleep from my eyes just in time for the door to open. Crank came in carrying two steaming cups of coffee, and a paper bag.

"Is one of those for me?"

He grinned. "Of course. I thought you might need some fuel." The side of the bed dipped a little as he sat and passed me one of the cups. "I brought you breakfast, too. Just glazed donuts, since I wasn't sure what you liked, so I hope that's okay." He dropped the bag at my side and reached for me with his now free hand, brushing his fingers over my nipple.

Heat shot straight to my core, but he pulled back far too soon.

"We have things to do. First, you call off work. Then we'll go over all the details of what you've found, and figure out what to do from here." He opened the bag of donuts. "Here, eat. It's a long fucking day ahead of us."

I sort of expected Crank to be all affectionate after we ate, and I certainly wouldn't have objected, but he just told me to get dressed. As soon as I did, he pulled a laptop from his bag and logged onto the hotel's wi-fi.

Did he regret last night? Was that why he didn't want to make love again? Well, I had to admit, it was hardly fair to him.

He made the earth rock for me, and I gave him the same thing he could get for a few bucks on any street corner. Of course he would rather wait. So I took a deep breath, determined to be a big girl, and get on with business.

Before he could get started on anything else, I told him about Sennit visiting my parents last night. "I have to get them out of town. They're going to be at the airport at noon, so I need to get with a travel agent and book them on a cruise, beyond his reach."

"We can take care of that right now." He asked me a few questions, got their info, and before I knew it, he had them booked on a cruise that would keep them away for a week. "Okay, now tell me everything you know about your boss. Names, dates, everything." While I talked, he typed, clicked, and typed some more. Then he read a while. The longer he read, the deeper his frown became. "Did you know Jared Sennit has a juvie record for sexual assault? Well, charged, but not convicted. The girl recanted. Can't believe I missed this shit when I started looking into him for Fabio."

"Are you serious? How could that happen? They run all sorts of background checks before we're hired." My mind raced with the implications. If he assaulted someone as a teenager, who knew what he was capable of now? Well, the girls in his case files knew. "Are you sure it was him? How did you find out?"

Crank looked up at me and gave me a devilish smile. "Let's just say I have ways. There's nothing you can't find on the Dark Web."

"Dark Web?" That sounded ominous.

"It's an unregulated part of the internet, basically. Anything can be had, including drugs, sex, and information. So even a sealed Juvie record can be had."

I considered that information. I'd heard of people getting drugs on the internet, so that must be how they did it. "So what's our next move?" The question assumed he would choose to go ahead with helping me, yet I couldn't be sure when he might decide he'd done enough, and just leave.

His shoulders lifted in a small shrug. "That depends what you want to do."

"What do you mean?"

"Well, I can make him back off and leave you alone, for one. Or we can make him choose to resign, and go elsewhere. Want to ruin him professionally? Or see him brought up on charges?" He grinned. "Or he could just...disappear."

"Why would he disappear?"

That grin came again. "He might decide he likes the weather in Alaska better than here. Or maybe he has a friend in South America he wants to visit. Or maybe he'll just walk away one day, and never be seen or heard from again."

"Oh." Or maybe Crank would kill him. For me. The thought didn't curdle my blood the way it should have. In fact, it gave me an odd sense of comfort. Was that how Tanya felt with Trip's protective nature? "I definitely want his ability to hurt kids taken away, so he needs to be ruined professionally, in a way that means he never works with kids again, not in any capacity, anywhere." I thought for another moment. "And he needs to pay for what he's done, so he needs to face charges."

"Okay, then. That's a starting point." He started to come up with specifics on how we could handle Sennit, without involving any children, and still avoid bringing in any direct supervisors.

I had to admit, the plan covered all the bases, and left no space for Sennit to wiggle free. We had him. "I love it!"

"Okay, I need to make a couple calls, and later we'll

probably have to go talk to some people face to face. Once we have everything ready to go, we'll have to contact someone much higher up in your agency, someone with no reason to coddle Sennit." He leaned back and stretched, making his muscles stand out against the thin fabric of his t-shirt. My mouth practically watered with the desire to taste him, but at the moment, he seemed interested only in business.

I sighed. Okay, I could do that for a little while longer. "That someone will be hard to find. He's a good politician, and he goes to all the conferences and meetings. He's been invited to the Governor's mansion for events several times, too. I'm just not sure who we could go to."

A speculative look crossed his face. "I guess we could go straight to the Governor, then. That'll take a little time to arrange."

That made no sense. "Why would the Governor help us?"

He shrugged. "He might not. But those invitations probably came from staffers, not the Governor himself, but it still associates him with Sennit. And most politicians at that level have higher ambitions. A hint of scandal like that in his state agencies, especially involving someone he's been in direct contact with socially, would kill any prospects he might have. So he can help us, or we can take it directly to the news media."

"That might work." It seemed like he had everything planned out. It all made sense when he explained it. Yet I couldn't help the sense of foreboding that prickled my spine. What were we missing?

He stood, towering over me, and gave me that devilish smile of his again. "Don't worry. It'll work." One fingertip stroked over my cheekbone. "Sit with me while I make my calls?"

He didn't need to ask twice. The craving to be near him startled me with its intensity. Before, when we first met, I thought the strong attraction I felt for him came from his bad boy edge. He was nothing like the men I normally found appealing, so it made an odd kind of sense. This time, though, I had no excuse. Crank made me feel things I always discounted as fiction, made up to sell books and movies, and whatever those things were, I found myself needing them desperately on some basic, essential level.

He sat on the bed, his back up against the headboard, long legs sprawled before him, and drew me to sit between his thighs, leaning against his chest. He dialed his cell from memory, rather than selecting a contact, and waited for someone to answer the call.

"Yeah, man, it's me. All good back there?" After a short pause, he went on. "Yeah, I'm good. Enjoying the vacay. Hey, you know that ol' boy we ran into out west a few weeks back?" Another pause. "I'd like to touch base with him. Think you can make that happen?" After another moment, the call apparently ended.

Crank threaded his fingers through my hair, and dialed someone else. "Hey man, I'm in our book cover Brother's old stomping grounds. Need some negotiation tools. Set it up." He dropped the phone onto the bed. "Now we wait."

How were those calls supposed to help? They sounded more social than anything. Had I made a mistake in calling Crank? "What are we waiting for?"

"Call backs. One of the Hell Raiders will set up a meet with a club we know in this area. Hopefully, when they hear what's happening here, they'll agree to help us. Another Raider is setting up a deal for some weapons. I couldn't bring much of anything on the plane." He chuckled, his breath tickling my neck.

"Weapons? Why?" Surely he couldn't mean guns? I mean, I knew he often carried one, and probably knew how to use it. But this was hardly the kind of situation that led to shootouts. Was it?

"Darlin', your boss won't give up his little money machine easily. You take into account he's low enough to rape kids, and all bets are off. There's no telling what he'll bring at us." He seemed to sense how tight my shoulders had become with the tension and worry, because he started working the knots loose with his thumbs. "Don't worry, though. This ain't my first rodeo. No matter what he does, I'll find a way to counter it, and keep you safe."

A chill settled into my spine. Was Sennit really capable of killing to protect his criminal acts? I hardly knew Crank, so could I really trust him with something this big and important? Sure, my life could be endangered, but all those girls Sennit victimized meant far more to me. If my life became the cost of keeping them, and others like them, safe, then so be it.

CHAPTER 7

Crank:

Even lying safe in a bed, wrapped in my arms, Sarah was fucking scared, and she should be. She might not have put this thing into terms of life and death before, but she sure had now. Fear tightened every muscle of her lithe body, and as much as I wanted to reassure and comfort her, I fucking refused to lie to her. By choosing to go after her crooked boss, Sarah put herself into a world of danger, and the only way out was to bring his ass down hard.

With a little luck, my plan would work out in spades. Unlike Sarah, I seriously doubted if Sennit acted alone in his activities, so I already had my sights set on any associates. He already proved himself willing to barter a child's innocence for his precious kickback by ordering Fabio's niece and nephew placed with what we now knew was a pedophile. In my experience, sick fucks like that usually sought safety in numbers.

For the time being, though, my biggest battle lay in keeping my fucking hands off Sarah. Before, I fucked her like I would never see her again. Things changed, though, and I wanted to see a whole lot more of her. If I scared her off now, I might never win her trust. Despite the raging need to burn myself into her mind and body, to mark her as mine, I worked hard to keep a little distance. That hadn't stopped me from stocking up on condoms when I went out for coffee and donuts, though. And I planned to use every one of them, but the time needed to be right. She deserved more than to have me go at her like an animal.

Her tense muscles slowly relaxed under my fingers, and she yawned—which I found adorable. Eventually, Sarah dozed, leaving me to think my outrageously dirty thoughts. The things I wanted to do to her would make a whore blush. I liked to fuck as much as any man, but this new, driving need threw me off balance. A compulsion to possess her, consume her, and mark her as my woman in a way that left no doubt made my heart race.

I tried to force my mind back to the situation facing us, and refine the plan to bring down Sennit and his kid raping buddies, with absolutely no fucking luck. Every time I started to think about how to lay my plan out to Fergus, Prez of the Ghost Walkers, fantasies about Sarah's body jumped in to distract me.

Fuck. I needed my head clear for this meet. The Walkers were a substantial club of mostly Native Americans, with a broad territory, and their hands in just about every pie. Operating on their turf without their approval, and assistance, would prove impossible. Last time, we managed to just notify them of our presence, but we had the necessary manpower to do the job. This time, I needed some of their people in the game. I just hoped to fuck they would commit to bringing the bastard and his buddies down.

I went over my plan again, searching for loopholes and weaknesses. Sennit was the loose cannon. I needed to know how he would react when things started going south for him, and he fucking figured out his days were numbered. He would make trouble. Of that, I had no fucking doubt. But he could easily hurt an innocent in the process, and I wanted to avoid that. Collateral damage always turned into bad press for MCs, no matter the surrounding circumstances.

Sarah shifted in my arms, turning to snuggle her cheek into my chest. A soft smile crossed her face. What was she thinking, or dreaming, to give her that smile? Was it about me? I fucking hoped so.

What the hell was my fucking problem? I never cared about how a woman felt before, or whether they were happy or not. And now I found myself hoping I put a smile on a chick's face while she slept. Fucking pathetic. I hadn't even properly fucked her since I came back. Hell, I'd barely got her off at all before I lost myself. I never had an issue with control before. I could fuck as long as the chick let me, and beyond, but with Sarah, I had to consciously hold back from the moment she opened her sweet mouth to me. Even now, just thinking about it, my dick hardened with need for her.

Shit. I spent the next few minutes trying to get my mind off Sarah—nearly impossible with her cuddled in my arms. No matter how silky her hair felt between my fingers, I had to keep my shit together. The risk to Sarah scared the fuck out of me. If I slipped, she could get killed, if Sennit had the balls. That thought turned my stomach and made me want to crawl inside her. Yeah, I couldn't handle losing her. I would have to do whatever it took to keep her safe, and preferably in my bed for a good long while.

She moved a little, roused up, blinking at me with sleepy, sexy eyes. That soft smile settled on her lips again, and something loosened in my chest. That smile was mine.

"Mornin', sleepyhead." I tightened my arms around her when she would have sat up. "Nope, you're not going anywhere. Got you right where I want you."

The smile changed and her teeth sank into her full bottom lip. "Oh, really?"

I tilted my hips a little so she could feel my hard-on. "Really." If it was the last thing I ever did, I had to have her again. The decision wasn't even fully formed before I flipped her under me, and settled my mouth over hers. The moan she gave in response loosened that thing in my chest a little more. I didn't take time to analyze it, though. To hell with waiting for the right time.

Sarah's mouth softened under mine, and she opened willingly for me. I refused to hurry. I spent a long time exploring her mouth, learning all her secrets, before I moved to her neck. Absolutely everything, like how when I ran my tongue along the shell of her ear, she whimpered with desire, I had to know it all. Ever fucking bit of her. Like how my teeth raked over a pulse point made her groan with need, and arch against me.

Clothes refused to melt away, no matter how much I wanted them to, so I had to take the time to remove them, but when they were gone, and I could see and touch all of Sarah's naked glory...well, the effort was worth it. As much as I sought to learn and explore her, Sarah returned it all in spades. This woman possessed the ability to fucking rock my world with just a touch.

The moment I slid inside her, I knew. The thing in my chest uncoiled with an explosion of awareness. How had I fucking missed this before? She was *it*. Destiny, fate, what the fuck ever you want to call it. That's what Sarah was to me. In the few short moments before I spilled myself into her, my whole universe turned inside out. It was no longer just me against the world. I had Sarah now.

She clung to me after, as we both struggled to catch our breath, and I wondered if she felt it, too. How the fuck could she not? I rolled to my back, keeping my arms around her, and pulled her as close to me as possible. Was I supposed to say something? Tell her? Or wait? After some consideration, waiting seemed like the way to go. If she didn't realize it yet, my saying it out loud might scare her away. What I felt was too fucking intense, unnatural. I couldn't risk losing her so soon. So I stayed silent, and let my touch say it. The messy condom needed taken care of, but I didn't give a shit at the moment, as long as she stayed in my arms.

The phone rang, breaking the spell, but I was tempted to fucking ignore it, and just stay there in that hotel room for eternity, holding my woman to me, keeping her close and safe. That call might provide the key to a future without fear for her, though, and I couldn't let that pass.

"Yeah."

"Hey, man, boss got you a meet an' greet with that ol' boy. Texting you the deets." Dix ended the call, having said all he needed to.

Sarah looked up at me, her face still flushed from sex. "Everything okay?"

Her lips drew me in before I could answer, and I lost long moments exploring them again. Finally, I managed to pull away. "Fucking perfect, now. Kellen managed to get me a meeting with someone who can help, if he will."

Confusion darkened her eyes a little. "I thought you said we shouldn't involve the police or anything yet."

I chuckled a little. "Darlin', these boys ain't cops." My phone buzzed with an incoming text. I checked quickly. "Shit, we have to get moving. The meet's in two hours."

"Oh. I guess you'll have to get ready, then."

"Not just me, darlin'. You know the details about Sennit. They need to hear it straight from you." Besides, I wasn't fucking letting her out of my sight. These men were not my Brothers, and therefore, not to be trusted with my woman.

A faint crease appeared between her brows. "Are you sure? I mean, I'm not usually that great around non-police types. They all think I want to take their kids away."

Irresistible. I smoothed my thumb over that little frown. "These guys won't think that."

"How can you be so sure?" Worry tinged her voice.

"For one, they don't actually live right here. And two, they're kind of a law unto themselves." Should I prepare her a little more for the Walkers? No fucking clue how to do that, though. They were...unique. Only one brief meet-up with a few of them left a lasting impression on me.

"That doesn't matter. Most people don't like caseworkers, or trust them."

Well, I couldn't deny that fact. "You'll have to trust me, okay? They wouldn't have agreed to a meet if they were going to hold your job against you. Kellen filled Fergus, the Prez, in a little, and he's agreed to consider putting his club's resources behind us to bring down Sennit. But he'll want to talk to you himself, too."

She paled. "Club? As in biker gang? Like yours?"

"Motorcycle Club. Just some folks who enjoy riding bikes. Whatever the individual members get up to is not related to the Club. Remember that." That little technical difference had to be drilled into her head. "And yes, kind of like the Hell Raiders."

She shook her head. "I can't be associated with criminals, Crank. I'll lose my job."

"They are not criminals. Neither am I." That hurt a little,

but I had to admit, some of the Walkers were probably up to their fucking necks in crime, just like some of the Raiders. I stepped over the line sometimes, but I tried to mostly skirt the legal bullshit. Fucking prison held no appeal for me.

One hand lifted to lay along my jaw. "I didn't mean it that way, Crank." She sat up. "I guess it's just that I know you, and feel safe with you. I don't know those people, and I'm nervous."

She felt safe with me? "Darlin', you shouldn't feel too safe around me. I'm the big bad wolf, ready to eat you up." I leaned to rake my teeth over her throat and growl a little.

She shuddered in reaction. "I don't think that's such a bad thing." She tilted her head, baring her throat more to me.

A sense of power, unlike anything I ever experienced, raced through me. Nobody *ever* trusted me that much. Ever. I could break this woman, and she trusted me not to.

Fuck the time. I grabbed a fresh condom and pulled her under me and slid inside her with one deep thrust. She wrapped herself around me and held on tight as I drove us both over the edge of ecstasy again.

CHAPTER 8

Sarah:

I tried my best to keep my nerves from showing as we rode to meet with Crank's friends. It all seemed surreal. Everything. From having Crank come to me, and having such incredible sex with him, to going to a meeting with a biker gang. No matter what he said, I couldn't turn off that phrase in my mind. They certainly weren't Boy Scouts.

Almost an hour later, we pulled into a parking lot outside a small bakery. I blinked at Crank in surprise. He wanted donuts at a time like this?

He smiled at me, and my bones melted. "Come on. Time to meet Fergus and his boys."

My heart sank into my stomach. "Here? At a bakery?" The idea seemed ludicrous.

"Yeah, here. The Walkers own the bakery and several of their women run it." He got out and came around to open my door. "Just stay beside me, and be ready to answer some questions."

My hand shook as I put it in his and let him help me down from the big SUV. Suddenly, Sennit and his thugs looked far less dangerous. Crank settled his warm hand on my lower back, and the fear subsided as he guided me inside. He wouldn't let anything happen to me.

Delicious aromas competed for attention inside, and a glass display case held an assortment of beautiful, intricate cakes. Another display brimmed with more kinds of pastries and donuts than I'd ever seen in one place. One section held nothing but cupcakes of unimaginable variety. Behind the counter, a refrigerated case held cakes and pies waiting to be picked up.

"This place is incredible!" I stared around at everything, unable to take it all in.

"Hi, welcome to Betty Blue's. Can I help you?" A redhead who looked like a 1950s pinup model smiled brightly from behind the counter.

"Yeah, we'll have the daily special." Crank didn't miss a beat, as if he came there all the time.

"Sure thing, sugar. Right this way." She came out from behind the counter and wove between the tables with a strut like a model on the catwalk. The smile she sent Crank meant he could have whatever was on *her* menu.

Jealousy surged through me, and I moved closer to Crank, plastering myself to his side. He glanced at me with one dark brow raised, then his gaze traveled to the waitress' butt, and he gave a knowing grin, but draped his arm around my neck. His big hand hovered just over my breast, reminding me of the sensations he could create with it. It felt natural to slip my arm around him and let my hand rest at his hip.

We reached a set of double doors marked 'Private', and the waitress halted and turned to face us. She took in the way Crank's palm practically cupped my breast, and smirked. "Wait right here. Someone will be out to show you in." She turned to go, but paused at my side. "I like it both ways, sweetheart. Just let me know if you need anything." She winked, then sashayed back the way we came.

My heart skipped a beat and I gasped as her words registered. Had that woman really just propositioned *me*? Heat surged to my cheeks as one of the doors opened.

"You're from Kentucky?" The skinny young man with the scraggly beard standing in the door looked us over doubtfully.

"Crank. Kellen told me the daily special here is really good."

The man nodded. "Come on." He turned to lead us through.

Crank leaned down to kiss the top of my head. "Stay close, darlin'."

I nodded. He didn't have to tell me twice. My stomach turned flip-flops as I took in our surroundings. We walked down an aisle created by pallets of supplies, all stacked higher than my head. The cool, dry air was at least a welcome relief from the heat outside.

The low light shielded most of the details from me, but I felt Crank's body coil with tension. Then we reached the end of the aisle and turned the corner into a large open area. A heavy plank table sat in the center, surrounded by an assortment of camp chairs, stools, and other makeshift seating.

The men sitting at the table drew my attention more than anything. Although they all wore the black leather vests and jeans Crank's buddies favored, the similarities ended there. Dark bronzed faces with penetrating black eyes turned our way. The men all had dark hair, ranging from blue-black, to dark brown, but while some wore military style crew cuts, long braids rested on a few shoulders. One man, large and imposing, had thick, blue-black hair surrounding his shoulders in a silky-looking curtain.

Two sported shaved heads, except for a circular patch at the crowns of their heads. The remaining section of hair had been allowed to grow long, and woven into complex plaits that swung to nearly waist length. Those two stood, somber, with arms crossed over their chests, behind the man who wore his long hair loose.

All of them were heavily tattooed, and wore what appeared to be bone piercings in ears, eyebrows, noses, and lips. I couldn't imagine a fiercer looking group of men. The man with his hair down rose to stand, hands on hips, and for the first time, I noticed what looked like a bone breast-plate, like some Plains Indians warriors wore before Europeans came along.

"You must be Crank." His voice rumbled, deeper than I expected.

"I am. And you must be Fergus."

"Truth. And who is the enchanting creature at your side?" The man's feral smile sent a chill up my spine.

Crank chuckled. "Down boy. This is my ol' lady, Sarah. She's also the one with the information on the dirty social worker."

Ol' lady? I tried to remember how Crank's buddies used that term.

Fergus laughed aloud. "You can't blame an Injun for trying." He returned to his seat, and motioned Crank to sit, as well. He sent one of the others to find a proper chair for me. "How can we help? And what do you offer in return?"

I sat there, feeling conspicuous and extremely uncomfortable, while Crank outlined Sennit's operation, and his plan to take it all down. The meticulous thought process behind the idea astounded me, but the feeling of overlooking something huge persisted.

Crank bargained with Fergus for what seemed like hours before a deal was struck. Finally, though, they stood and clasped forearms, then returned to their seats. Relief settled in, and my shoulders relaxed a little, until that nagging little doubt returned. What had I missed? There had to be something.

Fergus turned to me. "Okay, Sarah. Your turn. How do I get a girl into your system where this asshole can find her?"

Well, there it was. The big glaring hole in the plan. "I, uh, I'm not sure." I looked to Crank in panic, then explained. "Sennit knows I'm on to him. Any file that originates with me will be suspicious. I don't know how to get her in without putting her at risk." It was a nice thought, anyway. Bringing down someone who used the system to profit was one thing, but to stop someone who used the same system to victimize innocents? That was vital. And now we had no way to do it.

Crank shook his head. "So the file doesn't originate with you. Tell me exactly what happens when a new case file starts. How does a kid end up in the system?"

I spent the next half hour walking him through everything from the initial complaint call and investigation, to the child being placed. Once he realized how it worked, Crank would admit the loss. Nothing could be done without compromising anyone attached to this hypothetical file. But as I explained, he made a few notes on a pad, and nodded a lot. The men around the table half listened, and occupied themselves with more interesting pursuits, like cleaning their nails with huge hunting knives.

I finished, and Crank tapped his pen on the notepad for a few seconds. "Okay. I need the full names of everyone who works in your office."

"How does that help?" Yes, maybe I should just hand over the information he asked for, but those people were my friends and coworkers. I owed it to them to not just hand their information over without question.

Crank flashed me a smile, one I recognized from when

we took Fabio's niece and nephew from the home where Sennit
ordered me to place them. It came when we sped away from
the house in my work car, and I demanded he stop and let me
out. He told me he intended to keep me alive, whether I
wanted him to or not.

"Sarah. I need the names. With them, I can hack the
system and initiate the case under someone else's credentials.
I'll be able to backdate everything, so our file gets immediate
attention."

When he explained it that way, it sort of made sense. So
then why did I still feel like some astronomical base was still
left uncovered? "Okay. I'll give you everything I know on them
all."

"So there we go. The girl will be as safe as we can make
it, considering Sennit's actions of the past. And you know
exactly how it'll be done." Crank stood, and clasped hands with
Fergus again.

A heavy door closed loudly somewhere out of sight.
Fergus nodded and one of his silent shadows faded away into
the darkened area off to the side. All the men at the table
stood, and drew weapons.

With a huge gun in one hand, Crank took my arm with
the other, and pulled me close. "If I say the word, you run like
fuck back out to that bakery, get in the SUV, and get the fuck
out of here. I'll meet you back at the hotel." He pressed the key
fob to the rented vehicle into my hand and kissed my forehead.

Oh, God. What was happening? My heartbeat thudded
in my ears and sweat broke across my upper lip. Were we
under some kind of attack?

A male voice called out in an unfamiliar language, and
one of the men replied. The man who had run off into the
darkness returned, another man at his side. The pair spoke to

Fergus for several minutes, but since they didn't use English, I had no clue what they might be saying. For all I knew, they could be plotting to kill us, or sell us into white slavery, or something equally terrible.

Finally, Fergus finished his conversation and returned to his chair. "Crank, my brother, it is a very good thing my scouts are so good. Your gut told you true. Your hideaway at the hotel is compromised."

"Well, then I guess it's good I brought my woman and all my toys along with me, huh. Your scouts happen to get an ID on the intruders?" Crank seemed entirely undisturbed by the whole thing, but the calm I had begun to recover threatened to evaporate completely.

"You underestimate us. They did even better, and brought one of them back for you to speak with. I'm told he's extremely anxious to cooperate as soon as possible." Fergus repeated the same feral smile from earlier, and I could easily imagine him leading a war party to raid an enemy encampment.

My little shudder of apprehension didn't escape notice, and Fergus turned that smile on me once again, but said nothing. I was incredibly grateful for Crank's presence, because without him, I had no doubt that man would change from the almost friendly biker gang president to a terrifying individual. Even without Crank's order to stay at his side, not even a herd of wild horses could have pulled me away from him. I had plenty of dream nightmares without spending time alone with a real live one.

Crank smoothed his thumb along the inside of my upper arm, out of sight, in what I hoped was meant to be a comforting gesture. "Well, the bastard can wait a little bit. I'm going to get Sarah settled in a new location first, and make sure she's safe. Then I'll talk to him about his cooperation."

He said his goodbyes and draped his arm over my shoulder to lead me back along the corridor created from supply pallets. "Keep walking, no matter what. We need to get you out of here."

I certainly wasn't going to argue.

CHAPTER 9

Crank:

I practically shoved Sarah into the SUV and got behind the wheel. I couldn't get us out of there fast enough. At least one of Fergus' scouts would follow, and probably more, so I needed to take Sarah where they couldn't, or wouldn't, follow. Now where the fuck might that be?

"That was, um, interesting." She sounded small, frightened.

"That's one word for it." I risked a glance in her direction. "You weren't scared?"

She laughed. "Terrified. Those men looked very intimidating, but I felt like what lay below the surface was much more of a threat.'

"That's a good way of putting it, and very accurate." No trace of a tail showed in the rearview, but that meant nothing, really. "Fergus and his men are associated with other clubs we know, and sometimes work with. Kellen says Fergus is a straight shooter, but I don't know the man personally, and I don't fucking trust anyone other than my Brothers."

"So we can't trust him?"

"No further than you could throw him. However, he's a tool, and we'll use him. But he gets absolutely no further information until he proves he's actually on our side." A blue Taurus hung in the rearview, three cars back. Nothing made it stand out, but the fucking car made me itch. It was exactly the kind of car, and in exactly the position, I would choose to tail someone.

"What do we do now?" Her knuckles turned white where she clenched her hands in her lap.

I considered a little more. "Well, I wish I knew. There really isn't a place where Fergus can't go, or at least, reach, even though I fucking wish there was. It would make things a hell of a lot easier." The blue Taurus turned at a corner. Looked like I was wrong. A green Jeep took the car's place and I continued on down the street. "So, I think we'll find the fanciest, most exclusive hotel in the area, and check in."

"But...okay." She fidgeted, running her thumb absently across the back of her opposite hand.

I reached over and grabbed her hand, and drew her fingers to my mouth. After a quick, sharp nip to the pad of her index finger, I swirled my tongue over the tender skin. "But what?"

A little sigh escaped her. "I can't exactly afford fancy and exclusive. My budget runs more to Motel Six. I have a credit card, though—"

"Whoa. Wait just a fucking minute. You thought I meant you had to pay?" Annoyance flushed my face with unexpected heat. The very concept just floored me.

"Well, it is my problem. I'll just put the hotel on my card, like I did the other one." Her other hand clenched and unclenched in her lap, betraying her conflict.

"No, you fucking won't. I have more than enough cash on me to cover a few nights at a hotel, darlin'." There was no fucking way I would let her go into debt over this shit, especially not with over twenty-grand in cash lining my pockets, and more available.

Sarah pulled her hand away. "You aren't the one who got

in over your head. It isn't your responsibility to pay the costs. Any expenses involved are mine."

"Fine." If she wanted to think I would fucking let her pay for anything, she could dream on. But for the moment, I was more interested in the green Jeep back there, which had just whipped into a parking lot, and been replaced by the same fucking blue Taurus. "Motherfucker had us tailed."

"You mean someone is following us?" All that annoyance melted away with new fear. "Why would he do that?"

"Maybe providing us some security, or he might be worried he's being set up. Who knows? Whatever, I don't fucking trust him enough to tell him where we're sleeping."

"You say that word a lot, don't you?"

"Which word?" I played the last few minutes of conversation back in my head, and came up with nothing.

"Never mind. If you don't trust him, why are we including him and his people in this?" Okay, she was definitely getting annoyed with me, judging by the tone of her voice.

I barely managed not to sigh, aware that would really piss her off. "Because we need fucking help bringing Sennit down. I don't have any other connections in the area that might be able to give us the kind of help we need."

"We could still go to the police. They could help."

That fucking sigh about choked me, trying to get out, but I held it. "Sennit grew up in the area, right? Knows a lot of people?"

She nodded. "Yeah. He likes to brag about being the fifth generation of his family here. He played ball in school, too." She talked with her hands when she was frustrated, and I found it fucking adorable. "But I don't see what that has to do with getting the police to help. I understand about not going to his superiors. That would be too risky. But the police?"

The blue Taurus in the rearview switched out with the green Jeep again. Motherfuckers. "What are the chances that he went to school with, dated the sister of, played ball with, or whatever, at least one of the cops?" I glanced over long enough to catch the blank stare she sent my way.

"I don't know. Probably pretty high, I guess."

We approached a corner with a gas station that had double street access. At the last second, I whipped the SUV into the lot, floored it, and we jolted out the other side on the cross street. The green Jeep sat blocked by a minivan trying to leave the gas station. Perfect. Okay, then. "He knows you're on to him. He'll be leaning on every single resource he has, including people he played ball with, for information and favors. Evidence would disappear, along with witnesses. We would get nowhere, and Sennit would just continue business as usual. Only, when a particularly sweet little piece hits the system, he might share her with one of his cop buddies, to repay him for his troubles." I took another quick turn, hoping to shake Fergus' scouts for good.

Sarah sat silent for several minutes, processing everything I'd said. "Do you really think the police officers would do what he wants? I mean, I know he's friends with them, and the risk is there, but do people really do that?" Doubt of her own instincts filled her voice.

I nodded. "Absolutely. I've seen it a million times. He would take a twelve-pack over to the cop's house one evening, and explain how this bitch at the office is trying to screw him over because he broke things off with her. The whole woman-scorned defense. The cop knows him. He's a good guy, with a solid rep. Of course he wouldn't do anything wrong. And when the woman comes to the department with her story, that cop would make it all go away." One more quick turn, and still no sign of the green Jeep, or the blue Taurus. I set a course for a really nice-looking bed and breakfast place I'd noticed on the way into town.

"But surely there would be some of the police who would investigate?" The defeated tone of her voice made me wish I didn't have to explain how shit like this worked. It was bad enough she knew about it from TV shows and that kind of thing.

"It's possible. But even if there was an investigation, the cop who drank the beer with him is going to make shit disappear. By that point, he has to cover his own tracks. If he allows evidence to come up against Sennit, he's risking being outed as a dirty cop."

Sarah let her head fall back against the head rest, as if exhausted. "I can't believe I didn't know this kind of thing. I mean, I've wondered how it happened. Some pillar of the community beats his kid, and we investigate, remove the child, but they're quickly sent right back home. It all just goes away. And that's how it works."

"Yeah it is." I hated to be the one to tell her how the real fucking world worked, but she needed to know, too. I took the turn to the bed and breakfast. "When we get here, we sign in as Mr. and Mrs. Smith. The owners will know that's fake, but it doesn't matter, as long as they get their money." I chose the private place specifically because it was less likely to share information. Fucking chain hotels put everything in a central database, which someone like me could easily break into.

"People still do that? Like on TV, when someone's having an affair?"

I chuckled at her innocence. "Yeah, they do. But in a world where everyone pays with plastic, and everything is digital, it's getting harder and harder to use an alias like that.

So we go to a privately owned place, not part of a chain, and we pay cash. Some managers will even skip registering a guest in that situation."

"Oh." Apparently, it took some time to let all that sink in, along with the information about why we had to have help from Fergus. She stayed quiet, staring out the window, until we pulled into the circular drive at the bed and breakfast.

I parked under a big oak tree in hopes the spreading limbs would shield the SUV from view a little. We were still in Fergus' fucking town, and no doubt, he would quickly find where we were staying, but I didn't have to just hand it to him.

"Wait here, doors locked. Do not, I repeat, do not, open the doors to anyone but me. If I'm not out in ten minutes, you get behind the wheel and get the fuck out of here."

"But, where would I go?" The way her eyes widened with fear made my fucking dick twitch with want.

I thought about that for a second. She fucking trusted me, and as wrong as it might be, her fear combined with her trust in me to keep her safe made me want her all over again. "You look up the nearest FBI field office, and go there. Tell them everything."

She gave me a serious nod, and I got out, and waited to hear the locks engage before I walked up on the porch of the sprawling house.

A discreet sign directed me to reception as I stepped inside, and a bell on the door jingled. "Just a second!" The female voice came from the right, where the foyer opened into a big great room. A heavily pregnant woman with a pronounced limp came through and greeted me with a bright smile. "I'm Chancey. What can I do for ya, hun?"

The damn cheerfulness was contagious, and my grin refused to be contained. "I need a room for a few days, or a suite, if you have one."

In a matter of minutes, I had a suite for Mr. and Mrs. Smith, and knew Chancey's entire family history. She didn't bat a lash when I asked to keep things anonymous, as if she received similar requests all the time. Once she gave me the key, and the schedule for meals served in the dining room, I went back out to the car for Sarah and our things.

Inside, Sarah marveled at the house as we found our room. The carved moldings and vintage wallpaper fascinated her. I probably wouldn't have noticed more than the place being clean, but her delight with the glass doorknobs made me smile. I used the big iron key Chancey gave me to unlock our room, and stepped back to let Sarah go in first.

She froze in the doorway. "Oh, my God! Crank, this place is incredible."

I moved closer to see what astounded her so much, and felt my own jaw drop a little. Hardwood floors gleamed, but my attention went immediately to the huge carved bed in the middle of the room. Snowy white linens contrasted sharply with the dark wood, tempting me to throw Sarah right in the center, and fuck us both senseless.

I led her into the room, dropped our shit on the floor, and kicked the door closed. When she would have continued looking around at all the marvels, I lifted her in my arms. "You can check all this out later. Right now, I need you in that bed."

She smiled a little. "I thought you had to go back and see that guy they found?"

"That motherfucker can wait a few more minutes. I can't." I lowered her onto the bed, and bent to claim her mouth as I started pulling our clothes away.

CHAPTER 10

Sarah:

Crank left me dozing in the bed, both exhausted and surprisingly refreshed. At first, I thought sex with him was so different because of the danger he represented. The thrill remained, possibly from the situation as well as the man, but every time with him was more incredible than the last. Now, I found his touch becoming as essential to my existence as air.

God, I was such a fool. The thing with Sennit would be resolved, and Crank would go back home. I knew for certain he was not the staying kind, not the type of man to settle with one woman for the rest of his life. And yet there I was, dreaming about having him forever.

Reluctant to move and disturb the blissful feeling he left me with, I lay there for a while, trying not to think too much. Finally, though, a full bladder forced me up. The big claw-foot tub had a ceiling mounted showerhead, and a lush curtain hung from a brass rail to completely encompass the tub.

The thought of hot water proved too much temptation. The smell of lavender from the silky French-milled soap surrounded me, relaxing my muscles even further, if that were possible. Guilt over the amount of hot water going down the drain eventually forced me from the shower. I wrapped the thick cotton towel around me, and went to dig through my bag for clothes.

The persistent buzzing of my phone sent me diving onto

the bed, searching for it amongst the crumpled covers. My mom's name on the screen brought panic to surge through my veins. Had Sennit done something more?

"Mom?" I waited, breathless with fear. Had he reached them before they left?

"Oh, hi, honey. I just wanted to tell you our flight landed, and we're at the hotel now. I still can't believe this! Are you sure you can afford it all?" She sounded happy and excited, completely unaware anything might be wrong.

My pulse calmed a little, and I smiled. "I'm sure, Mom. I just wanted to do something really nice for you and Dad." Thoughts of maxed out credit cards tried to intrude, and I resolutely pushed them away. Debt meant nothing compared to my parents' safety. It was a small price to pay for keeping them in one piece.

"You could have saved for your wedding and honeymoon, though. You'll want it to be very special. Your young man is so dashing and handsome!" She gushed a little more about Sennit.

My stomach rolled. There was no need to lie more. "Listen, Mom, I have to tell you, it isn't like that. I'm not dating Jared Sennit, or anyone else from the office, and never gave any indication I might want to."

Silence stretched for a moment. "Nonsense, honey. You don't have to pretend with me."

I sighed. Time for the truth, now that they were safely out of his reach. "I'm not pretending, Mom. Jared Sennit is corrupt, and he's a predator. That whole little charade was a message to me. I've been digging into the corruption, finding proof, and through that, I stumbled onto something much bigger. He was telling me to back off and keep quiet, or he would harm you and Dad." I held my breath, waiting for her reply.

"Honey, you really don't have to do this. We know you're not supposed to get involved at work, but—"

"Mom! Will you listen to me?" Frustration made my chest heave. "I'm sorry. I know you'd like for me to be settled and raising a family. But Mom, I'm telling you the truth. Jared Sennit is taking kickbacks to place children in certain places. He's raping girls in return for good placements. And that could only be the start of it."

"Oh, honey..."

"That's why I had to get you and Dad to go away quickly. Him coming to the house was a direct threat. He had my apartment broken into, and sent a threatening text. I need you to stay away until he's arrested and charged." Telling her so much was a risk, but one I had to take. They couldn't come back here right now, even if they did think I had gone off my rocker.

"You can't do this alone, honey. Turn it over to the police and let them do their job."

I swallowed back a sigh. She always thought I was too fragile to do any kind of dirty work. "I'm not doing it alone, Mom." I tried to come up with a quick explanation for Crank, without giving too much information away. "The guy I'm working with is an expert, and he's making sure I'm safe, too, so you don't have to worry."

"Oh. Is he an FBI agent?"

My inward laugh came out as a little cough. Crank might not like the impression I gave of him. "Something like that. He and his associates know what they're doing. They do this kind of thing all the time." I crossed my fingers to keep the lies from counting.

Mom sighed, and a little thrill of triumph shot through

me. She was going to give it up. "Honey, you know I have to tell your Dad. He knows people. He can get it all looked into and settled."

"No!" Dread broke a cold sweat over my body. "You can't do that, Mom. Or rather, Dad can't. You can't do anything that might jeopardize our case. Too much risk and too much work have already gone into it. If Dad starts asking around, Sennit will pick up on it."

"Well, honey, I can't help it. You're obviously in over your head. Dad can help."

Anger, unlike any I ever felt before, overcame me. All my life, every time they thought I was 'in over my head', Dad came rushing to the rescue. It had to stop. "Mother, listen to me." I never spoke to her that way, but it was too late to take it back.

"Young la—"

"No. Listen, Mom." The indignation in her tone nearly stopped me, but fear forced the words out. "If you interfere, if Dad interferes, in any way, you will be putting me, and other people, in danger. I can't live with that. I know you want to help, but I have to handle this on my own. The best way to help is by keeping yourselves safe, and staying away until I get this taken care of."

"Now don't be angry, honey. You know we just want to help." The placating note in her voice failed to lure me in. She signed. "Honey, just promise me you'll be careful. Do what the FBI agent says, and stay safe."

"Mom, I know you want to help, but this isn't a playground spat, it's my responsibility, part of my job, and I'm taking care of it. Please trust me." Tears stung my eyes. The most rebellious thing I'd ever done in my life was choosing to go into social work. My parents tried to make me change my mind, but I held firm. I finished my degree, and made one small concession by accepting a position in my hometown. Telling my mother to let me handle this came in at a close second on the Channing Rebel Scale.

"Okay, honey. I trust you. We'll stay out of town until you put the son-of-a-bitch in jail." Was that pride in her voice?

"Thank you, Mom—" A low sound out in the hallway interrupted my train of thought. "I have to go now, but I'll call you soon. Love you, and tell Dad I love him, too." I ended the call and shoved the phone in my pocket while rummaging through my purse for the gun Crank gave me.

Blood thundered in my ears, but the unmistakable sound of careful footsteps continued. The gun felt cold and heavy in my hand, but I held it the way Crank showed me. Were you supposed to pull something to make it ready to work? All the TV shows I'd seen involving guns said yes, but Crank had said all I had to do was point and pull the trigger. Maybe there were different kinds of guns? I decided to follow Crank's directions, and hope he knew what he was talking about.

My bare feet made no sound on the polished wood floor as I hurried to the door and put my back to the wall just beside it. The doorknob rattled a tiny bit, and if I hadn't already been paying attention, I would have missed it. Something shifted on the other side of the heavy wood door, and the faintest scrape of metal on metal reached my ears. The wall felt good and solid at my back, and I waited, reminding myself to breathe.

The glass doorknob turned silently, and I clutched the gun closer, and pressed my shoulders harder against the wall. The door swung slowly inward and I waited behind it, my breath frozen in my lungs. What if Sennit had found me? He would be furious that I'd asked for help.

The floor creaked a little as a tall muscular man stepped into the room. Something over by the window seemed to catch his attention as he closed the door softly. Startlingly black hair hung straight to his shoulders, concealing his features from me.

I forced myself to swallow my fear. That would only get me killed, or worse. The gun felt even heavier in my grip as I raised my arm and pointed it at the man. It shook, so I used my other hand to steady my wrist. The man took another cautious step, still intent on something by the window.

"Don't move!" I put every bit of false bravado I possessed into those words. "I have a gun, and I'll use it."

The man froze and lifted his hands away from his sides.

"Who are you? Who sent you?" Did my voice really sound that small and terrified? My whole body throbbed with the force of my heartbeat.

He shook his head, but stayed where he was.

I tried a deep breath, forcing air into my lungs and praying for courage. Crank. I needed to get Crank. The gun wavered as I let go with my other hand and dug my phone out.

"Yeah." Crank answered on the first ring.

Relief rushed through me, turning my bones to jelly. "Oh my God, there's a man. He broke in—"

"Fuck! Who is he?" The command in Crank's voice helped me get hold of myself a little.

"I don't know, he won't say. I'm making him stand still and I have the gun."

"Mother fucker. Okay, you stay out of reach, keep that gun pointed at him, and I'll be there in a minute." He ended the call, leaving me to panic.

The big man started to turn, slowly. "Look, I'm not here to hurt you."

"Right, you just broke into my room just because. Don't

move." I steadied my gun hand again, careful to keep the weapon pointed at his chest. The man glared, but kept his hands up and stood still. "Who are you?"

He shrugged and grinned. "Don't matter. You gonna get your ol' man killed, waving that thing around." He nodded to indicate the gun. "Better just put it away right now."

Well, he couldn't very well kill Crank while I held a loaded gun pointed at his chest, could he? I smiled. "I'll take my chances. Who sent you?"

He sighed. The man actually *sighed*, as if he were bored. "We both know you won't pull that trigger. Just put it down."

The words shook me a little. Would I? If it came down to my life, I didn't know. But if Crank were in danger, I had no doubt. I would blow that man away. "You're wrong. Who sent you?"

He smiled. "Whatever." In a flash of movement too fast for me to follow, he jumped at me and wrenched the gun out of my hand. Sharp pain slashed through the tip of my finger as a nail broke.

I struggled against his grip, but he held me immobile, one arm around my waist, my hands both trapped over my head in his other hand.

CHAPTER 11

Crank

Tires screeched as I ignored traffic and pulled a tight U-turn. The big SUV surged ahead when I stomped the gas pedal, and quickly pulled away from the blare of horns. Sarah's panic on the phone had me swerving through traffic with no regard for law or safety. If something happened to her, nothing else mattered.

Who the fuck could have broken into the room? And why? Sennit? One of his cronies? One of Fergus' men? Or someone from a totally different direction?

If the fucker hurt Sarah, he would wish for Hell Fire before I finished with him. The depth of my anger might have shocked me if I took the time to examine it. But right now, the only thing that mattered was how it pounded through my veins and drove me to get to Sarah, no matter what.

Finally, I skidded the SUV into the lane of the Bed and Breakfast, and nearly took out the porch rail with a sliding stop. The .45 comforted me a little as I pulled it out of my belt, ready to destroy any threat that popped onto my radar. The SUV's engine ticked as it began to cool, annoying me. I should have come in quiet, but it was a little late for stealth now, so I didn't bother.

The main rooms on the lower floor held no one. For a second, I wondered about Chancey. I'd hate for her to get hurt in this mess. Every damn stair tread creaked under my boots, so it was a good thing I didn't give a shit about being quiet. Whoever broke into that room on Sarah had to know I was coming, and he had to be ready for me. Fuck it. Didn't matter.

I topped the stairs with enough presence of mind to take a quick look around for threats, right before I planted my foot next to that pretty glass doorknob, and busted the lock to pieces. The door flew back and hit the wall behind it, hard, then rebounded toward me, but I caught it on my shoulder and pushed through. The bastard stood between Sarah and me, blocking my view, so I had no idea if she were okay or not.

He turned to face me, and grinned. "I was starting to think you left your woman to handle me on her own." He held Sarah pinned against his chest, practically immobile.

The fear in her face nearly broke me. No risk was too much to guarantee her safety. Now who the fuck was this bastard? "What do you want?" I kept my gun barrel centered on his head and eased sideways, desperate to at least touch Sarah.

He kept his arms around her, clearly aware of the .45 zeroed in on his head. "Just some words, man. Nothing more."

Where the fuck was her gun? "Let her go. She has nothing to do with this." My molars threatened to crack with the pressure of clenching my jaw.

He gave a slow nod, then loosened his arms. "Okay. I just want to talk."

Sarah jerked away from him and ran to me. I wanted nothing more than to wrap her in my arms and keep her safe forever, but I had to settle for pulling her against me with one arm, while I kept my gun on the intruder with the other. "You're okay. I got you now."

She nodded against my chest, no tears, or sobs, or anything like that. Pride surged through me. My ol' lady had some fucking balls. "He didn't hurt me."

I let Sarah go long enough for a quick pat-down, which turned up a 9mm and a knife. "You got a funny way of asking for a parlay." I studied his face, trying to remember if I'd ever met him, and came up blank, though he did seem slightly familiar. "How about you start with who the fuck you are?" I kicked the door closed behind me and went on into the room, skirting around the intruder.

"They call me Runner. Fergus tells me you want to send one of our women into the state system to help you catch a low life." The guy shrugged and looked very uncomfortable. "I want in."

"What do mean, you fucking want in? You're not a chick that could pass for fifteen. Sorry to break that news to you, man."

"Okay if I sit?" He tilted his head toward the pair of easy chairs in front of the fireplace.

"Go ahead. But don't fucking waste my time here. I got shit to take care of." If this idiot knew how to ask to talk like a man, instead of dragging a woman into it, I would already be questioning the fucker Fergus' men caught.

He sat, leaning forward, elbows on knees. "Look, man, this...You can't tell a fucking soul what I say here. Yeah?"

One look at the misery in his face convinced me. "Yeah. It goes fucking nowhere, man. Now, what's up?"

He dropped his head into his hands for a second, then straightened. "Okay, so my mom was white, you know? I lived with her 'til she got busted for trafficking when I was eleven years old. They didn't have no way to contact any other family, so I went into the system." He paused to run his hands over his face.

I raised a hand to keep him quiet for a second. "Hey, Sarah, you think that chick would have something cold to drink downstairs? I could sure as fuck use a beer." If anything this guy had to say even remotely resembled what I feared it did, I didn't want her to have to hear it.

Her eyes went wide for a second, then she nodded, hopefully catching my hint. "I'll go see."

The door closed behind her and I turned back to Runner. "Okay, man, go ahead."

"Thanks, man. This shit ain't easy. So, I went into the system. The first home I got was good. The people took care of us, you know? But after a while, the caseworker said I had to move. New place was bad, and I acted up. When I got in trouble, another caseworker said if I wanted to go back to the good place, I had to do what he say. I didn't have no idea what he meant, man." He stopped and took a deep breath, trying to calm down.

The sick feeling that started in my gut the minute he started talking kept getting worse. "You remember this caseworker's name?"

"Jared Sennit. He was brand new at the job, and he did everything his boss told him to. Fucker named Mark Carson."

I listened while he told me all of it. How this bastard got him moved to a better home, but Sennit picked him up from school once a week and took him to a hotel. Every week, a different man waited at the hotel to rape him. By the time he got to that part, I really fucking needed that beer.

"My dad finally tracked me down, got me the fuck up out of there. He put Carson down, but the chance to get Sennit never came. You're going after him, and I want in."

"A'ight, man. As long as Fergus gives the go-ahead, you're in. And don't forget, I'm calling the shots." I waited for his nod of acknowledgement. "Let's go see if my ol' lady found that beer." The rage coiling in my gut demanded action, but for now, I had to wait.

Runner confirmed my suspicion that Sennit shared his victims with other sick fucks. Not only that, but he fucking turned them out, and it looked like kids, boys or girls, of just about any age, suited him just fine. The only thing worse than a pedophile, in my opinion, was the one that served the kids up to be raped. That right there took a special kind of slime, and Sennit ticked off the checkboxes. Fucker needed to die.

The doorway into the kitchen downstairs revealed Sarah and Chancey talking by a big butcher block table, with several bottles between them. Sarah looked up with a big smile. "There you are. I asked Chancey about beer, and she was just filling me in on the local brewery."

Chancey gave her infectious grin. "My sister and her husband are the owners, so I have more beer around than any pregnant woman should." She went on to show us the bottles.

Personally, I'd have been happier with a plain old beer. Instead I got a fancy bottle of craft beer that tasted more like piss.

After the first taste, Runner stalked past me and poured his beer down the drain. "Must be a bad run. That shit is awful."

Chancey giggled, one hand over her mouth, the other resting on her big belly. "I thought it was just me. Everybody talks about how good it is, how different, and act like a bunch of snooty wine experts. I think dirty dishwater would be better."

Mine went down the drain, too, even though Sarah shot a frown my way. "You're too damn nice."

No actual drinkable beer showed up, so I suggested to Runner we should go on about our business, and leave the ladies to chat. I pulled Sarah aside for a quiet word. "I'll be back in a couple hours. I'll fill you in on what that was all about when I get back." The way her body yielded into mine as I drew her close for a kiss ensured I wouldn't stay gone one second longer than necessary. Turning to go, I lifted a hand to Chancey, and caught her fanning her flushed face. "Chancey? You okay?"

Her fair skin flared brighter. "Oh yeah, fine. Just suddenly a little warm in here. You two could make a living as a furnace."

Unable to smother my grin, I headed for the truck, glad to hear Sarah's laughter behind me. Runner already waited in the passenger seat. Odd. I'd have figured he'd have his own wheels. "What you do, walk all the way out here, man?" I cranked the ignition and the big engine turned over.

"No, my ride hauled ass back home. By now, she standing in the barn munching on some grain." The sideways look he sent my way seemed like an attempt to see if I took him seriously.

"Don't tell me you rode over here on some swayback mule, man. I'd lose all respect."

The gauging look turned to a grin. "Have Mercy is the finest damn quarterhorse in the county. She'd kick my ass for letting somebody call her a mule, or swayback."

In other words, our intruder made sure he left behind nothing that could be tied to a name and residence. Fucker probably didn't have a scrap of paper on him, either. These days, with digital fingerprint and facial recognition technology, those precautions didn't mean a whole lot, but they still showed awareness and commitment.

It didn't make much sense to bother with taking a roundabout way back to the bakery to talk to the fucker Fergus' scouts picked up, considering I had one of his boys sitting right next to me. The drive only took a few minutes without the worry of being tailed, and we pulled in at the front of the bakery. Place didn't seem to have much traffic at the moment, so I parked in the same space as before.

One of Fergus' men met us just inside, before I had to ask the girl at the counter. "Come on back, Crank. Some of the boys been keeping your guest all comfortable." He nodded to Runner. "Good to see you, boy. Figured you'd hear about this and want in."

We followed the man back through the labyrinth of bakery supplies. Fergus and his boys had a guy sitting on top of the table. I assumed this was whoever they caught poking around the hotel where I met Sarah. The fucker looked distinctly uncomfortable.

Runner went forward. "Dad." He offered a hand to Fergus.

Well, hell. No wonder Fergus was willing to put his people at risk for a problem that really had nothing to do with him. Since it seemed like one of Sennit's victims was Fergus' kid, I had no fucking doubt he wanted Sennit's blood. I sure as fuck would, if I were in his place.

"Crank." Fergus lifted his chin in my direction. "I see my boy found you."

"He did, just as I was headed out this way." Not a good idea to mention the exact circumstances, I figured. It wouldn't do anyone any good to make Runner look less of a man to his dad. Especially not me.

Runner grinned. "His old lady got the drop on me at first."

Fergus laughed. "I knew that pretty white lady had some steel in her backbone." A few minutes spent teasing Runner led to my introduction to the guy on the table. "Crank, this boy calls himself Jesse James. I guess he figured that name gives him the right to be an outlaw. He should have played cowboys and Indians a little more."

I turned my full attention to the bastard Fergus' scouts caught. "Mr. James, I know these boys been real nice and entertaining, but I ain't got time to fuck around with your stupid self. You tell me what I want to know, first time I ask, or I hurt you. Last feller pissed me off good had a nice home-cooked supper of his own balls. You don't want that shit to happen to you."

The fucker on the table wasn't alone in turning green. "What did you wanna know?"

"How about you start with Sennit raping kids?" Half an hour later, I had everything he knew about Sennit and his operation.

CHAPTER 12

Sarah:

Chancey placed a big mug of herbal tea in front of me, and sat across the table with her own. "Okay, you have to tell me. Where do I find a guy like yours?"

My gaze automatically went to her big baby bump. "I met him through work, entirely by accident." The words for how to explain, without revealing details that could give up my identity, came slowly. "His friend was in the area on family business, and he came along for moral support."

Her eyes widened. "Was it romantic? Of course it was romantic. Just look at the man." Her hand rested on her belly again in what seemed like a habit. "I have two more weeks until this baby comes. As soon as I hand her over to my sister, I'm going to make some changes. I have to at least get out more."

The thought came out before I could stop it. "You're not keeping the baby?"

Fortunately, Chancey seemed not to take offense. She offered a broad smile. "No, she isn't mine. I'm just carrying her for my sister and her husband. They've lost so many, and the last time there were complications that meant no more tries for them."

The generosity of her gesture struck me. Could I do the same thing for someone else? Even a sibling? I wasn't so sure.

"So what kind of changes are you going to make?"

The tea mug partially hid her nervous smile. "I'm not sure. I might even sell this place, start over somewhere else. Nothing ever changes around here. It's the same people I grew up with, only they've moved on from being jocks or troublemakers to being used car salesmen and criminals."

I nodded. "That's exactly how I always felt about my hometown. My family always just assumed I would eventually settle with one of the used car salesman types, and give them grandbabies. They're going to have a fit if they ever meet Crank."

"You don't think they'll like him?"

A little laugh escaped me at the thought. "He's hardly the kind of man they would have chosen for me. I can see it now; my dad and Crank scowling at each other across the table while my mom tries to make small talk. It won't be pretty." Something else occurred to me. "Of course, that might never happen, either. He might not want anything beyond short term." My mind shied away from thinking of the devastation he would leave behind him.

"No, I think you're wrong there. From the way he looks at you, that man wants nothing less than forever with you."

Could she be right? And if she were, was forever with Crank what I really wanted? At the moment, I thought it was. How would I feel in a week? A month? Frustration welled up. How could I even know? "I'm not even sure what I want."

Chancey's irrepressible smile appeared once more. "You'll figure it out. And when you do, you'll wonder how you missed something so obvious."

"I hope you're right. I'm not used to being uncertain about things." A change of subject seemed like the perfect idea. "So, if you left here, where would you go to start over?"

We chatted on about the world of possibilities until Chancey's phone rang. I stood to leave and waved a little before going out onto the broad front porch. A cool breeze took advantage of the construction, and kept the temperature comfortable on the porch, despite the heat of the late afternoon.

I'd thought of it before, of course, but what would it really be like to just leave and go somewhere new? I didn't even have to consider how my parents would react to the prospect. Appalled, angry, and hurt were only the tip of the iceberg. They would do anything and everything possible to convince me to stay home, and I really couldn't blame them. They built a life on making the safe choices, and as I grew up, minimizing risk was one of the lessons they tried really hard to impress on me.

Did I want to live the rest of my life without taking chances? Could I actually leave the little safety bubble of home? The world was a big scary place, and I always had my parents to turn to when things went wrong. Could I truly go it alone? Or with Crank by my side? Everything I thought I knew about my future, and about life, seemed out of balance since meeting him.

Even scarier than the prospect of leaving everything familiar behind, was the thought that I scarcely knew this man. Basically, the force of his personality, and his sex appeal, held enough power over me to make me consider throwing my life away on the chance of a future with him. Clearly, I needed a plan. Before I could really consider any kind of long-term thing with Crank, I need to know so much more about him. I started a mental list of things to ask him about; politics, religion, and family were all huge parts of a person's identity. And then little things, like pizza toppings, ice cream flavors, and whether he put the cap back on the toothpaste also went on my list.

The door behind me opened, startling me a little, and Chancey came out onto the porch. "You come to any big momentous decisions out here?" She awkwardly lowered herself into one of the rocking chairs, making me smile.

"Only that I need to get to know Crank a lot better." Something about her open and honest nature made me want to confide in her. "I might have a little issue getting past the physical long enough to find out much about him."

Laughter spilled over. "Oh, I bet you do." Then she sobered. "But honestly? My momma used to say if the match works physically, everything else can be worked out."

Could it really be that simple? "I always thought I needed to know everything about a man before I could get serious with him."

Chancey stretched her feet out, and rubbed her belly. "I swear, this little girl is going to be the first female NFL player, the way she kicks. A lot of people think that way, but look at history. At one time, it wasn't uncommon for a couple to meet the first time on their wedding day, or to only see each other a few times before getting married. Then look at today, when people date for years, then get engaged for more years, and then get a divorce just a little while in."

I had to admit, she had a point. "I wonder why it works that way sometimes?"

"There's no mystery left, nothing special about being married, nothing really to look forward to. The adventure is over before they even commit to each other."

"You think so?" It made an odd sort of sense.

"I do. My parents got married just a few weeks after they met, and they're still madly in love after thirty-five years. My sister and her husband were engaged within a week of meeting, and married two months later. They just had their tenth anniversary, even after all the heartache they've seen with losing babies."

Interesting. My parents were engaged for two years, and while they seemed happy enough together, there were no sparks flying, or anything like that. It was like they were just comfortable with each other, but no longer really *in love*. Everyone else I knew had long engagements, and short marriages. Definitely food for thought.

The sound of tires on the lane interrupted anything I might have come up with to say in response. The sight of that big SUV approaching, bringing Crank back to me, sent my pulse skyrocketing.

Chancey grunted as she struggled to her feet. "Looks like your man is back. I'll let you get on with getting to know him." She grinned broadly. "If you need anything, I have my little place off to the other side of the kitchen. Just ring the doorbell." She opened the door. "Have fun." Her laughter followed her inside.

The SUV came to a stop a short distance away, and I waited impatiently for the engine to shut off and the door to open so I could see him clearly. After an eternity, Crank stepped out of the truck and strode to the porch. The way he moved held me mesmerized. This man never had a moment of doubt in his life, with confidence and discipline clear in every step.

My stomach tightened with anticipation as he came closer. God, I was hopeless, getting all hot and bothered just watching him walk toward me. By the time he stopped in front of me, my body was wet and ready, needing him.

He raised a hand to the pulse beating so wildly in my throat. "Mmm. You know what I love?"

"What?" How could a single word sound as if I were

throwing myself at his feet?

"I love the way your pussy is already wet and tight, waiting for me." He lowered his head and brushed his lips across mine. "Your nipples are hard, wanting my mouth on them." As he stepped closer, bringing me tight against him, heat exploded through my body. "You fucking rock my world, Sarah." His mouth was hard and hungry on mine, and he slid his hand down to cup my breast.

Powerless to do anything other than cling to him and return his kiss, I offered no resistance when he guided me backward. I hardly noticed moving until my shoulders encountered the siding of the wall behind me. Even then, I lacked the presence of mind, or willpower, to object when he lifted my shirt and sucked my nipple into his hot mouth.

Heat built rapidly within me, making my remaining clothes uncomfortably tight. Crank's fingers went to my waist, and before I knew it, he roughly worked my jeans down, and I could do nothing but help, and wait as he undid his own pants. Hard fingers clamped down on my hips and he lifted me so my legs automatically opened around him.

His hard heat brushed against me and created an instant firestorm, but he paused, instead of pushing inside me as I so desperately needed. "Sarah, look at me."

I forced my heavy lids up to find his intense gray eyes staring into mine. "What's wrong?" Worry tied my stomach in knots. Was it already ending? I wasn't ready.

"This is for-fucking-ever, Sarah. You are mine. Don't you ever forget that." With a heavy groan, he lowered me to give me what I needed.

The first thrust made lights explode behind my eyes, and then I lost the ability to do anything other than cling to him and wait for him to take us both to paradise. At some point, he shifted me a little and changed the angle of our bodies, intensifying every movement he made. And then the cresting wave of my orgasm crashed into me, and Crank followed closely with his own.

By the time I started to catch my breath, I realized where we were. On the front porch of a public business establishment. Where anyone could come along at any time. *Oh my God!* I squirmed to get away from Crank and pull my clothes back on.

His laughter rang out, rich and full, probably the most relaxed sound I had ever heard from him. Around that same time, his words started to sink in. Forever? His?

CHAPTER 13

Crank:

Following Sarah up that fancy staircase was one of the hardest things I've ever done. Partly because every single cell of me wanted to grab her, strip her, and fuck her again, right there on the stairs. And also because a big part of me was scared of how she would react to what I said out there on the porch. I sort of hinted earlier, but this was the first time I boldly declared my intentions toward her. She could easily tell me to fuck off. Probably should. But I prayed she didn't.

I opened the door to our room for her. "I guess I owe Chancey a new old lock, huh?" Yeah, anything but talk about the purple polka-dotted elephant in the room. Real fucking smooth.

"She said don't worry about it. Apparently, these old locks are a little temperamental, so she has several extras on hand." She shook her head, and looked up at me, eyes full of confusion and worry. "Crank, I don't know what's happening between us. I—"

"I didn't mean to push you."

"I don't even know you."

I shrugged. "I'm an open book. What do you want to know?" No, I did not fucking say that. Couldn't have. I didn't talk about my past, my family, for a reason.

"I don't know." She crossed to the chairs by the fireplace,

looking even more confused than before. "We haven't actually talked about anything really. When you were here before, it was the stuff with Nicole and Tyler, and now it's all about Sennit. Do you like mushrooms on pizza? What's your favorite milkshake? What kind of movies do you like?"

I went over behind her and tucked her hair to the side, revealing the column of her neck, and let my fingers trace the delicate skin. "I can take mushrooms, or leave them. I'm pretty easy to please with food. But I really don't fucking like green beans. Milkshakes, it's chocolate all the way. I'm easy with movies, too, as long as it's action or suspense. I read a lot, but mostly, I'm online. I keep music blaring in my office while I work, classic rock, heavy metal, old country, and a lot of other stuff. Now how about you?" The attempt to shift the focus off myself usually worked with women.

She smiled up over her shoulder at me. "Mushrooms are a must. Chocolate. And I don't like blood and guts in movies." Her fingers wrapped around mine and she tugged me to the chair beside her. "What's your real name? Tell me about your family, about growing up."

And there it was. The question I dreaded. "It's not a pretty story, Sarah."

"I'm not looking for pretty stories."

I sighed. "James Harrison Baer. It's an old family name. My daddy was a tobacco farmer, and ran his daddy's old moonshine still on the side, grew a little weed on the side of the side. Momma worked in a factory. I have two older sisters, and a younger brother. My sisters got the fuck up out of Stags Leap as soon as they were old enough. When I was seventeen, and my brother was fifteen, daddy's still blew up, and killed him. Momma drove her car off a bridge a year later."

"I'm so sorry." Her soft fingers rested against my jaw,

and she blinked away a tear as I looked up.

"It was for the best. Daddy was mean as fuck when he was drunk, which was pretty much all the time. Momma took the worst of it, but us kids still got the living shit beat out of us regularly." I took a deep breath, trying to hold the past at bay.

"Why didn't she leave him?"

"She wouldn't have made it out of the county alive. Daddy's ancestors were some of the first whites there, so whoever he wasn't related to fucking owed him for shine, or was afraid to cross him. She was from Michigan, but I don't know much of anything else about her family. They cut her off when she ran off with the hillbilly." Nausea curled in my belly, warning me to leave the subject alone. But my Sarah wanted to know, deserved to know. "After they died, my brother went to live with one of our sisters, but I stayed in Stags Leap. One of my teachers talked me into staying to graduate, and taking some classes at the community college a couple of counties over." Fuck, I needed a drink.

"Is that where you met Fabio and the others?" Her soft touch brought a hard lump to rest somewhere in the center of my chest.

"Second semester, after I finished up finals, I went to a party. I never had time for that shit, but a couple of the guys gave me a hard time about it, so I went. And after, I got in my old truck and started home. I took the back roads so I wouldn't get picked up in a road block sobriety check. Almost made it, too." God damn, that room needed more air. I got up and went to the window, heaving it open to gulp in deep breaths.

Sarah's hand on my shoulder pulled me out of the urge to fucking cut and run. "You don't have to tell me the rest, if you don't want to."

"Yeah, I do." It took me another minute to fucking

gather the courage. "I don't really know what happened. I guess I dozed off, or something. I woke up enough to fight them as they pulled me out of the truck. I killed a man that night. Old motherfucker out wandering along the side of the road. I never even got charged. Everybody knew it was a matter of time before he got hit."

"That doesn't sound like it was your fault."

My hands curled into fists. "Maybe. Maybe not. Either way, I needed a change. I enlisted in the Army. Did really good there. Loved my work. Then I got a new First Lieutenant. Fucker was a real hard ass. One day he pushed too hard, and I slugged him, and broke his jaw. Ended up getting put out. When I came home, I kicked around a little while, until Kellen approached me about some work. I ended up in the Club, and never looked back." I turned to look at Sarah, expecting the condemnation I deserved to reflect back from her face.

Except it wasn't there. "I'm sorry things were hard for you." And she fucking meant it. She smiled up at me. "Want to change the subject?"

I couldn't do anything but nod, as another piece of my soul became hers.

She led me back over to the chairs. "What did you learn while you were out?"

One more deep breath helped settle my fucking nerves. "Well, that guy, Runner? He's Fergus' kid. And while he was in the system, Sennit fucking pimped him."

A mixture of anger and horror settled on her face. "So this is a lot worse than Sennit molesting some nearly-legal girls."

"Yeah. A lot worse." I went on to tell her what I'd learned from the jackass Fergus' boys caught, but I left out how I persuaded him to talk. The less she knew of the dirty business

I did, the better.

"So what do we do now?"

"I'll hack into the system at your office tonight. Tomorrow, we see about getting our girl in there."

"Is it safe? I mean, I know it's not safe-safe, but what if he finds out we're using her to get him?" Worry made a little furrow between her brows.

Fuck, she didn't even know the girl Fergus picked to send in, and she still worried for her safety. "It'll be as safe as we can make it. She'll be armed, and wired up, and she's not a kid, even if she does look like one. Help will be close by in case she needs it, too." If I gave any indication how fucking dangerous this was going to get for that girl, Sarah would pull the plug right now.

"You're sure?"

"As sure as I can be. Not very fucking much is certain in this world." Seemed like the perfect time for a change of subject of my own. "You have fun while I was gone?"

That smile of hers fucking blew me away. "I did. Chancey is really nice, and she's hilarious."

"Good qualities in a mom." At least, it seemed that way.

"I'm sure they are, but she isn't going to be a mom, despite appearances. The baby is her sister's."

"Huh. So she's generous, too." Neither of my sisters would have done anything like the for the other. Most of the time, they were too busy competing against one another for something to even really notice they were sisters.

"She is. And she seems to think you hung the moon." Her eyes twinkled with restrained laughter.

"What?"

She told me about her conversation with Chancey. "You know, I've always made safe choices. Well, except two times."

"What choices did you make that weren't safe ones?" Tension began to knot my shoulders. I didn't know if I could listen to how some fucking quarterback broke her heart in high school.

"I went into social work. That was the first one. My parents were worried sick. They didn't want me around the seedier parts of life. To them, that sort of work wasn't for a woman, especially not a young one. But when it came down to it, every career choice out there has some less-than-desirable elements, which I pointed out as quickly as possible. Even though I shot down every suggestion they made, they were still incredibly disappointed with my choice. As far as they were concerned, I should have gone to school for an MRS instead of a Masters."

I thought I'd heard of about every degree there was, but that one was new to me. "MRS?"

"Otherwise known as a wedding ring." Distaste tightened her mouth. "A lot of girls go to college to husband hunt. Or at least, a lot I knew did."

"And you weren't interested?" Somehow, that didn't surprise me too much, but it made me happy as hell.

"I was much more interested in learning everything I could to make the world a better place."

Okay, I had to play devil's advocate a little, and see if I could get a rise out of her. Those little flashes of temper she sometimes showed were hot as fuck. Maybe I'd get lucky. "There's a lot of ways to make the world a better place, though. Everybody from teachers to cops to politicians list that as a fucking career goal."

The little smile surprised me. "True. But since I couldn't really become a superhero, I decided to be the next best thing. I'll save as many as I can, one kid at a time, from the bad things that go bump in the night."

"Well, fuck. I was trying to provoke you into being slightly pissed, so I could enjoy the view. Instead, you come up with something with real meaning."

She smiled and stood. "I know. So I decided to give you a different view." Her shirt came up and over her head in one smooth movement, then dropped to the floor, leaving me stunned with her beauty.

Heat flashed to my groin, even though it had only been a few minutes. Fuck, this woman turned me inside out. I couldn't get enough of her.

CHAPTER 14

Sarah:

The big house sat quiet, and mostly dark, as I led Crank down to the kitchen in search of food. It made me feel like a teenager sneaking around after dark, and I tried to control my giggles.

Crank caught on quickly, and cracked corny, dirty jokes until he had tears of laughter streaming down my face. When I would have opened the refrigerator, he caught me around the waist and pulled me back against his hard body. "I fucking love to make you laugh." With a quick nip to my earlobe, he released me. "Now, feed me, woman. I need fuel."

I turned to stare at him, a little startled by the change of tone. "Why?"

"Because I need to fuck you again and again." He leaned in to tuck my hair back. "I don't fucking know what you do to me, but I can't get enough of you. Every taste leaves me starving for more."

No appropriate reply appeared in my head in the next heartbeat, so I settled for the only coherent thought I could find. "Oh. Okay." The refrigerator yielded cold cuts, cheese, and fruit, while my brain continued on empty.

Crank found a jar of what appeared to be artisanal crackers made from some whole grain, but without a label, we couldn't be sure. He lifted one shoulder, unscrewed the lid, and tried one of the irregularly shaped squares. "Okay, I don't know what the fuck these are made of, but they're incredible." He added a generous handful to our haul.

In the absence of wine, we chose a cranberry juice blend. Glasses and napkins joined everything else on a wooden tray, which Crank insisted on carrying, and we made our way back upstairs.

I never considered food even remotely erotic until that meal. Watching him eat flipped some sort of primal switch in me, or something. Crank ate the way he did everything else, including sex—decisively and without reservation. We'd eaten together before, but I never watched with such fascination. And all the while, those gray eyes held me mesmerized.

Eventually, we finished, and when I would have taken the tray back to the kitchen, he stopped me. "It can wait for morning." He placed it carefully on a polished marble-topped table, which also held a large vase of fresh flowers. "Time to get to work."

I felt so stupid for getting caught up in the romanticism of being with him. "Yes, it is." Maybe my disappointment didn't show too plainly.

Crank put his laptop on the bed, and turned to face me. One thumb brushed over my lower lip. "Hey, the sooner we finish this, the sooner we can focus on more important things. Like the future."

Wild horses galloped through my chest. Did that mean—

"Come on, sit with me." He put his back against the headboard and patted the mattress beside him. "Once I'm in the system, it'll be faster if you guide me."

The wild horses evaporated. "Of course." I scooted back

beside him, but kept a little distance between us. This man confused me with the way he went from hot to cold so quickly. Which side was the real Crank? Would I even get a chance to find out before he rode off into the sunset?

As soon as the laptop finished its startup thing, he opened a couple of programs I didn't recognize. "You know if there are any other guests here tonight?"

The question seemed entirely random. "No, why?"

"Because if there are, they might come knocking to tell me to turn it down." After a few low, eerie, opening notes, a driving beat filled the room with heavy bass.

My eardrums recoiled in self-defense about the time a growling voice joined in. Reflexes brought my hands up to cover my ears.

"Too loud?" Crank's shouted words barely penetrated the cacophony.

I could only nod helplessly, and breathe a sigh of relief when he lowered the volume. "What on earth is that?"

"Marilyn Manson. Guess you need to be eased into some things. What do you listen to?" The way his brow arched betrayed his doubts about my taste in music.

"Pop. Taylor Swift is probably my favorite."

"I ain't gonna even fucking pretend to know who, or what, that is. But I have some classic rock that might appeal to you a little more. You've heard Tom Petty before, I'm sure?" That brow arched again, clearly expecting a yes.

I considered for a moment. "I don't think so. It doesn't sound familiar."

His face fell. "You're kidding? You haven't heard *Free Fallin'*, *Mary Jane's Last Dance*, or *Won't Back Down*?" He paused long enough for me to shake my head. "You been under a fucking rock your whole life?"

"Maybe? I don't know. My parents weren't music lovers, and I wasn't really either. I just listened to whatever my friends were into." Okay, those words made me feel like a fool, like someone who just blindly went along with the crowd.

He gave a little grunt. "Okay, then. Well, just so you know, I listen to everything from Hank Senior and Johnny Cash, to The Rolling Stones, Bob Seger, Pantera, Kid Rock, and Rob Zombie. So you'll hear a fucking lot of different sounds and eras of music around me. Tom Petty and The Heartbreakers hit big in the 80s, and their music is still relevant. Never know, you might even like it."

After a couple of clicks on his screen, an entirely different sound filled the room. It felt clean and pure, and the singer's voice fit perfectly with it. "Okay, I think I like this."

A satisfied smile curved his mouth. "Fucking told ya." With that issue settled to his satisfaction, he went to work, opening a browser window. His fingers flew over the keyboard and he clicked through screens so rapidly I had no chance of deciphering any of it.

The longer I watched, the more my respect for Crank grew. Unless I missed my guess, this man had the skills to work for the government, combating cyber-terrorism and things of that nature. Doubt followed quickly. Why would a man with so much talent and skill squander it on petty crime? He'd mentioned work before, but gave no details. If he didn't work for the good guys, exactly *who* did he work for?

The question burned in my mind, becoming more insistent with every sure keystroke. "You mentioned work before. What do you do? Like programming, or something?" It sounded intrusive, and lame, but I managed not to apologize for asking.

"I do a lot of things, consulting mostly." His pace never

faltered. "Sometimes it's coding, setting up a website. Other times it's security, or even banking."

The reply piqued my interest. "Who hires a computer consultant for banking?"

He glanced my way with a little grin. "Whoever has the money to pay, and wants to."

A deliberately vague answer. Did that mean criminals hired him? Memories of crime documentaries flooded my mind, details of how mob accountants had been found dead, and others turned evidence and went into witness protection. "Are you in danger because of it?"

His hands froze over his keyboard, and he turned to face me. "No. Even if, for some reason, they were unsatisfied with my work, they couldn't find me. I work from behind layers of encryption the NSA would have to work hard to get through. I don't even use a fake name. Instead it's a series of randomly generated numbers embedded within an avatar that looks like abstract modern art."

I considered that. "But then how do you get paid?" Surely money had to change hands, right? And money was traceable.

"Bitcoin routed through several anonymous accounts. Can't be tracked." He explained briefly how it worked. "You don't have to worry. No kill squads breaking the door down at night, or anything like that."

I still had my doubts. "Okay, I think."

He leaned in and stole a quick kiss. "I fucking love it when you worry about me." And just like that, he went back to work. The speed with which he shifted his focus startled me yet again.

More questions flooded in, demanding answers, but I held off. The last thing I wanted was to make him think I questioned his integrity, or something like that. So far, he'd patiently explained things to me, but that could change. I already knew he possessed a deep sense of honor, and strong, unwavering morals. So what if his ethics were a little different from those of mainstream society? It didn't change who he was.

After what seemed like hours, he spoke again. "I'm in. Ready to walk me through it?"

"Of course." We spent the next hour with him entering the details of our fictitious case report.

He took careful notes of everything. "In the morning, we'll go over all this with our girl until she knows it as well as she knows her own life story. You'll need to prepare her for what to expect, too. Fergus says she's never been in the system before. Runner will help prepare her, since he knows how it works from the other side." He clicked a few final checkboxes. "Okay, submitting now."

My heart leapt into my throat as the little circle spun on his screen. "Oh, God, I hope this isn't a big mistake."

Crank started shutting down his computer. "It's not. This is the cleanest, surest way to bring Sennit down. Now that it's rolling, we just have to follow through, and make sure it all goes exactly as planned." He set the laptop aside and scooted around to face me fully. "We'll fucking get the motherfucker, Sarah."

I nodded. "You're right. It just seems counter-intuitive to me. My instincts keep wanting to go to law enforcement with what I already have, and turn it over for them to handle. But logically, I know that has zero chance of working." This went directly against my normal rule-following tendencies.

"Not to mention, going to the cops would put you, and your family, at risk. Don't forget, he's already moved against you." A gentle finger tipped my chin up so I met his steady gaze. "A dirty cocksucker like Sennit will have a contingency plan."

"Contingency plan?"

"Yeah. He would know there's always a risk someone would find out. He'll have thought it out in advance, and have a plan to either discredit, or silence, anyone who stumbles across his dirty secret."

"Oh. That's what he was doing with me." The now-familiar fear flooded my system with adrenaline. "I almost wish I'd never found out."

Crank shook his head. "No you fucking don't. We don't know how many kids he's raped and sold over the years, but we do know it's more than a few. We also know there would be a fucking lot more before he stopped on his own. You want to make the world a better place, this is how you do it. You make sure that motherfucker can never hurt another kid." The ferocity of his words chilled the air. He took this as personally as I did.

"I know. I guess I'm just scared. It's just...I'm trained to spot abuse, to remove children from unsafe situations. To think I have handed children over to this monster's depravity—"

"No. Do not fucking go there." His fingers cupped my jaw roughly. "This is on Sennit's head, not yours. As soon as you spotted it, you investigated, and when it got too big for you handle, you called in help. *No one* could have done more." His touch gentled. "Now, I want you to forget about Sennit. I fucking need you again, Sarah." Eager hands removed my clothes and drew me into his lap.

Just like that, my doubts dissolved. As soon as he touched me, I knew all I needed to know about him. I gave myself over to the force of nature that was Crank.

CHAPTER 15

Crank:

Nothing in this world compared to waking up with Sarah all soft and warm in my arms. It made everything right, and I never wanted the moment to fucking end. I lay there, inhaling her scent and absorbing every single detail. I needed her burned into my mind forever, so I could never lose her, no matter what life brought at me.

She eventually stirred a little, then stretched, all satisfied, like a cat with full belly and a fire to curl up beside. "Mmm. I need to get up."

My hold tightened reflexively. "No, you don't."

Her eyes fluttered open, and a soft smile curled her mouth. "Yeah, I do. Otherwise, I might pee all over us both."

I grinned and held on a little longer. "That doesn't sound so terrible. But I guess I'll let you up."

As soon as I released her, she bolted from the bed and dashed for the bathroom. A couple minutes later, the shower came on. I headed for the bathroom to take a piss, and hopefully catch a glimpse of her, all slick and wet.

I eased the shower curtain back a little, and stood there, fucking stunned. How could one woman be that fucking beautiful? Suds rolled down her back and over her ass, teasing me. Throat too dry to make a fucking sound, all I could do was watch her.

She turned to rinse her hair, and swept her gaze over me with a smile. "You like what you see?"

I could do nothing but nod.

"Well, are you going to just stand there?"

I didn't need to be told twice. I stepped into the tub with her and let the scented steam carry me to a different world. Dropping to me knees in front of her, I filled my hands with her ass and pulled her close. She opened her thighs for me a little when I licked her.

If I thought her taste compared to paradise, the unique blend of both of us was something far beyond that. Yeah, I'd ate other women out after sex, but I could take it or leave it. This, the way her body mixed our come together, was a fucking drug. I would never be able to survive without it.

I groaned into her, searching for more, and sent her over the edge. Her nails dug into my shoulders, while her body trembled over me. Reluctant, I drew back as her orgasm faded and the sensation became too much for her, and got to my feet.

She leaned into me. "How do you always do that to me?"

"Do what?"

"Know exactly what I need, and when." A soft hand trailed down my abs, and lower, to circle the base of my hard-on.

I gritted my teeth as she slid her fingers along my dick with delicious pressure. "I'm going to spend the rest of my fucking life giving you what you need."

She paused for an instant. "Do you think it could work?"

Unable to speak further, I leaned down and took her mouth in the deepest kiss I could manage while I arched into her hand. She responded, open and honest, and found just the right pace with her fingers. It didn't take long for me to come unbelievably hard. Rather than draw back in disgust, my Sarah held my cock against her belly while I fucking spilled myself over her silky skin.

I finally managed to catch my breath enough to search for the washcloth she dropped when I came into the tub. Careful and gentle, I washed her while I thought about her question. Could it work?

Absolutely, it could. Should it? That was a different matter. I was pretty sure she owned me, heart and soul, but could I be the man she needed? I never imagined trying to leave my sketchy-as-fuck life behind. As badly as I wanted Sarah, needed her, I wasn't sure I could make that kind of change. Lucky for me, she didn't say anything more about it while we finished in the shower, and got dressed. I needed to seriously consider whether I could do it or not, before I took things much further with her. She probably needed to think things over, too.

Downstairs in the kitchen, we found Chancey at the big gas range, happily humming some tune I'd never heard, and cooking breakfast. She glanced up with a smile as we came in. "You're just in time."

My stomach growled loudly. "Good. I'm fucking starved."

Sarah gripped my arm a little. "Crank, language."

Puzzled, I looked from her to Chancey, and back again. "Darlin', I really don't think the kid will come out telling everyone to fuck off, do you?"

Her mouth twitched with humor even as she tried to look stern. "That's not what I meant, and you know it."

I leaned down to claim a quick kiss. "I know, but it's fun to fuck with you."

Across the room, Chancey sputtered with laughter. "Sarah, I think we had better feed him before he hurts himself."

"I think you're right. Have a seat, Crank. I'll get you a coffee and help Chancey finish up."

I followed orders and planted myself at the table where I could watch every move Sarah made. She brought my coffee, and leaned down for a kiss, and allowed me a little peek at her cleavage, then went over to the counter.

The easy interaction between the two women told me a great deal about them both. They were already well on the way to becoming close friends. They chatted as they worked, laughing often, and once, Chancey stopped and grabbed Sarah's hand to place it on her belly.

The look of wonder that spread over Sarah's face fucking blew me away. "Incredible! Oh my God, Crank, I felt the baby move!"

Fuck, that expression on Sarah's face made me want to plant my baby in her belly, and watch her carry it. I took a sip of my coffee, and tried like hell to keep my face neutral. "You want kids sometime, Sarah?"

She froze and stared at me, like a deer in the headlights, while I hid behind my fucking coffee mug. "I do."

My heart took off like a rocket. "Cool. You'll make a great mom." Where the fuck did that come from? Why didn't I just tell her I wanted my baby growing inside her?

"How about you? Are there tea parties and blanket forts in your future?" She turned away, back to the stove, but not before I spotted the fear on her face. Was she afraid I wouldn't want babies with her?

Another sip of coffee gave me a few extra seconds to consider how to word it. "I never even fucking considered the possibility of kids. I'm not exactly the carpool type, after all. But then something changed a couple months ago." A little more coffee. "Now? Yeah, I definitely want kids."

She brought a big dish of scrambled eggs over to the table. "What changed?"

I stole a piece of bacon from the plate Chancey brought over, and took my time eating it, before I answered. "I met you."

"Oh, God, Sarah, that's so romantic! If you don't want him, I'll take him." Chancey winked at me. "Okay, not really, but if there are any like him back home, I'm in the market."

I couldn't help but laugh. "There's actually a few like me back in Kentucky. Be careful what you wish for, though. None of the Hell Raiders are easy to get along with."

Both of the women sat down, Sarah beside me, and Chancey across the table from us. Chancey asked questions about the Raiders, and Sarah told her about those she met when we were there for Fabio. The delicious food kept me too fucking busy to talk, so I just observed while they chatted.

Full to bursting, I reluctantly pushed my plate back. "That was really good, Chancey. Thanks."

Sarah added her praise for the food, and offered to help clean up, but Chancey refused. "I've got it, hun. You guys go have some fun together."

"It'll only take five minutes if we work together. Then you would have a little time to rest." Sarah stood and started stacking plates, undeterred by Chancey's protests.

Yet another thing I liked about Sarah. Her kindness and consideration for others seemed as natural as her blonde hair. "While you're doing that, I'm going to go out and stretch my legs a little." I needed to take a close fucking look around the place while I had the chance. If Runner got in easily, anyone else could, too.

Sarah sent me a little smile over her shoulder. "Don't get lost."

"Not a fucking chance, babe. Gotta get back to my woman."

Outside, everything around the front offered a good line of sight all the way out to the road. Around the side of the house, I found a different story, though. The big place rambled, obviously added onto multiple times in its history, and several odd angles and corners turned into ideal hiding places for prowlers.

At the back was even worse. Some kind of fucking big flowery bushes were up against the house. A whole goddamn army could hide in those things. A little patch of overgrown woods also crowded up close to one corner, providing yet another way for attackers to get close. I hoped to fuck she had some kind of cameras concealed, but I couldn't find a single one, so I seriously doubted it. Totally fucking unimpressed by the possible defenses of the house, I went back inside.

Sarah met me as she came out of the kitchen. "I'm ready, whenever you are." She leaned up a little to accept my kiss.

The ride out to Betty Blue's turned into a sort of transition between the world of reality, where we had to deal with Sennit, and that of being absorbed in each other. I fucking preferred the one where I could focus everything on Sarah. The sooner I eliminated Sennit from the face of the Earth, the better.

Runner came out as I started to park the SUV, and approached. "Fergus wants us to take care of this part at his house. Better if there's no attention brought to this place, or the Walkers, so no one can connect her to us."

I considered for a moment. If Sennit happened to have a line on where Sarah had gone, he could already have someone watching us. If the girl we were sending in were seen with us, or in the same place as us, it could turn into a fucking disaster.

"Okay, that makes sense."

"I'll ride out with you, make sure you don't get lost." He climbed in the back seat. "Take a left out of the lot and make a left at the third light."

We left the town behind quickly, and the rural road we ended up on seemed entirely abandoned, at least for the time. "It always this fucking quiet out here?"

"Usually. Fergus controls all traffic on this road, from the last turn. Anyone not authorized would have been turned back there. That's how he can be certain no one connects any of us with the girl." He directed me through two more turns, onto smaller and more rural roads, until I took a right onto a lane that consisted of a pair of dirt tracks along a thin tree line.

The house, when it appeared, came as a bit of a surprise. I didn't know what I expected, but it sure as fuck wasn't what I found. The squat structure blended into the landscape almost seamlessly. Unpainted wood had weathered to a near-exact match to the broad open field surrounding it. The place looked like a stiff breeze would fucking blow it into next week.

"Pull in under the shed. He don't want cars or anything else to be visible from the air. Place is meant to look abandoned, and it mostly is. Only gets used a couple times a year."

I followed directions, silently admiring the forethought that had gone into the meeting. Fergus clearly knew the vulnerabilities of his surroundings. A few minutes later, Runner led us into a surprisingly nice living room, where Fergus waited.

CHAPTER 16

Sarah:

Fergus showed us into what could have been a living room in any nice home in the country. I clung to Crank's arm a little, because even though everything was clean and tasteful, a big part of me remembered that feral look in Fergus' eyes when we first met him. He wore the airs of civility, but deep down, his true nature sat watching for any opportunity. I didn't want to be anywhere in the vicinity when that came out.

"Crank, Runner, have a seat." He cast a predatory glance in my direction. "Lanea is waiting for you in the kitchen." And just like that, he dismissed me and sat at a table, indicating Crank and Runner should sit with him.

I tried to keep my hand from shaking as Crank grasped my fingers. He sat, tugging me into his lap. "Actually, if it's all the same to you, Fergus, I'd rather Sarah and the girl be included in our talks, too. Sarah has very real concerns for her safety, and she'd feel better hearing what we plan to do to make sure this comes off successfully."

A faint hint of annoyance flashed over Fergus' face, concealed so quickly I thought I might have imagined it. "Of course. We wouldn't want your woman to worry." Even I recognized the dig at Crank's masculinity in the tone. "Lanea. Come in here."

Crank grunted. "Considering I intend to hold onto my woman, and not lose her to some fag preacher, I don't want her worried either."

Whatever that statement meant, the impact on Fergus was clearly visible. "Point taken."

A slim girl of about fourteen came in and stopped beside Fergus' chair. "Yes, Uncle." Shining black hair swung loose to her waist, accentuating delicate bronze features.

"Lanea, these are the people I told you about. The woman works with the man who hurt your cousin. She's worried about you."

Startling gold eyes flashed to me. "No worries. I get the cocksucker that hurt Runner, I cut his balls off and nail them to the wall." A small, wicked-looking blade appeared from between her fingers. "He won't know what hit him."

Crank must have picked up on my shock. "How old are you, Lanea? Because you don't look fucking old enough to even be jail bait."

She glared at him for a second. "Twenty-two, but it doesn't matter. I would go anyway. This is family vengeance."

I stiffened my spine and prepared to deal with her like I would any other rebellious girl I encountered at work. "It might be vengeance for you, Lanea, but it's much more than that to a lot of kids. Sennit isn't doing this alone. We need names and information to get them all. Otherwise, he'll just be replaced, and nothing will change. If you can't work with the rules we lay out, we'll find someone else."

Her knowing smirk turned my stomach. "Don't pretend with me, lady. Fergus told me you work with that bastard, saw him doing this to kids. Why you suddenly want to help?"

A deep breath helped me stay in control of my anger. "Maybe I'm stupid, but until a few weeks ago, I never suspected he could be doing anything like this. Then I thought corruption, taking kickbacks for placing kids in certain homes, was the worst. If a girl hadn't told me what he did to her, I might never have looked further."

"Yeah, you are stupid as fuck. You give a man power over women and children, those weaker than him, and he *will* abuse it."

"Men don't hold a monopoly on abuse." Another deep breath. Arguing with her was counterproductive. "Can you follow the rules Crank and I give you?"

She rounded the table to sit beside Runner. "I can. You tell me what you need me to do, and I'll do it."

Runner laid a gentle hand on her arm. "Your word, Lanea. I don't want you getting hurt for taking stupid chances."

Lanea lowered her eyelids and her mouth tightened for a second. "My word. I will do as you say." When she looked back up at him, her eyes glowed with the sort of adoration a young girl might give a big brother. She would go to any lengths for him, including staying within the limits set for her.

Crank smoothed one hand along my back, easing a little of the tightness there. "Last night, your file went into the system. We don't have a lot of time to prepare you here. Someone could already be looking at the case now."

Runner nodded. "I have someone at the address we discussed. Since Lanea won't be at school where they can reach her, the caseworker will have to make contact there."

"Perfect." I gave a quick overview of what she could expect from the initial visit, and Runner filled in some details for her. "Now for the rules."

Lanea rolled her eyes. "I was hoping you would forget that part."

"Not a chance, girl." Runner squeezed her arm a little. "First, you'll be wired up. Someone will be watching and listening all the time in case there's trouble. You will also keep your little blades, but only use them if there's no alternative."

Blades? Something told me I didn't want to know, so I kept my mouth shut. Instead, I listened as Crank went over her background story with her. Within an hour, Fergus and Crank seemed satisfied, and we climbed back into the SUV with Lanea, and went back to the Bed and Breakfast.

Just before we arrived, Crank pulled into a gas station lot, and got out, followed by Runner and Lanea, while signaling me to stay in the car. Lanea went with a middle-aged woman wearing too much makeup and too few clothes in a beat-up car.

"Where is she going?"

Crank gave me a serious stare as he climbed back in the driver's seat. "We can't very well be seen anywhere near her. That lady will drop her off at the address we gave for her in the file. Everything there is already in place. For now, we go get a little rest, then check out after dark, and head back to your neck of the woods."

"We're supposed to just wait? And *rest*?" Impatience came through loud and clear in my tone.

"Yes, we are. Right now, doing anything else will only endanger Lanea."

That cut right through my objections. "Okay." I might not like her, but I certainly didn't wish any harm on the girl.

He drove us back to Chancey's house, and I started inside while he followed with Runner, the two of them chatting quietly. A harsh cry met my ears as I stepped up on the porch, and I froze, terrified.

Crank noticed my fear immediately. His breath warmed my neck as he spoke low in my ear. "Go back to the car and get behind the wheel. You hear shots, you get out of here fast and don't stop for anything."

I nodded, even though I wanted to go straight to

Chancey and help her. The rule-abiding part of me took over and I complied with his orders, while he and Runner started inside the house, guns drawn.

The guns did it. Shocked me out of any complacence I might have had. Somewhere in that house, a woman I considered a friend was in trouble of some kind. I had to do anything I could to help her. I sprinted back for the house, coming in the door in time to see Crank's back disappear through the door to the kitchen.

Another cry, more agonized than the first, came from that direction.

"Aw, fuck! Runner, get Sarah in here *now!*"

Crank's words spurred me onward. "I'm here. What?" I pushed past Runner and into the kitchen.

Chancey lay on the floor, in something like a fetal position as she gasped for air.

I flew to her side. "It's okay, Chancey, we're here now." I pushed her hair back and tried to soothe her. "Just keep breathing, honey." Vaguely, I realized Crank and Runner were turning her slightly.

"Keep talking to her, Sarah. The baby is coming now." Runner's low voice was probably intended to calm me, but it backfired.

"What do you mean, now? It's early. Call the ambulance."

"No time. Crank, I need towels." Just like that, Runner took over. "Talk to her, Sarah, help her calm down and breathe."

Chancey's shrieks of pain terrified me, but I pulled myself together. "Listen to me, Chancey, you're going to be just fine. Help is on the way. Now I need you to breathe, okay?" I just prayed the help arrived in time. I had no clue how to help anyone have a baby.

Chancey nodded a little, and gripped my hand hard. Crank returned with towels and dropped to his knees at her other side.

Runner spread a towel and helped Chancey raise her legs. "The two of you, hook your elbow under her knee and pull up toward her chest to give her leverage. Keep hold of her hands, too." He pulled her clothing out of the way. "Okay, Chancey, the baby is crowning. With the next contraction, push like hell."

I fought to help provide leverage as Chancey struggled to bring the baby into the world. Finally, with one last shriek, she collapsed back.

"Good. Perfect baby girl." Runner jostled the wet, bloody infant around, rubbing her roughly with a towel.

The tiny red face screwed up and a plaintive wail came out.

"Oh, my God! Chancey, you did it!" The incredible event I had just witnessed nearly overcame me. Tears flowed as I watched Runner lay the baby on Chancey's belly, while sirens cut through the suddenly quiet afternoon.

The next few minutes passed in a blur as the paramedics came in, rushed to take Chancey's and the baby's vitals, and loaded them onto a stretcher.

"Wait!" Chancey stopped them before they could wheel her out the door. She turned, until she found Runner and raised a shaking hand to reach for him. "Thank you. I was so scared."

"I am honored to help." He squeezed her hand. "If it's okay, I'd like to come visit you in the hospital."

Chancey nodded as the paramedics insisted they had to get moving.

In the quiet that followed, Runner washed up, while I cleaned the floor and put all the towels in to wash. Crank said something about needing some air, and went outside.

"Where's her man?" Runner's question startled me out of my jittery mood.

"She's single, and the baby is her sister's. Why?"

He shrugged. "Just wondering. A woman that far gone shouldn't be out here all alone. She'd have been in trouble if we didn't show up when we did."

"It wasn't supposed to come for a couple more weeks." For some reason, I felt like I owed him an explanation. "I'm sure she wouldn't have been alone if she realized it was coming so soon."

He gave another enigmatic shrug. "Babies come when they want to. Doesn't matter if they are human or animal. When they're done, they come out. She wasn't prepared to handle the birth herself, and her phone was nowhere to be seen. It could have gone badly."

The words raised questions in my mind. "How do you know about delivering babies?"

A rare grin flashed. "That was my first human one. But I've helped cats, dogs, a few cows, a lot of horses, and a pet rat."

I couldn't help but laugh. "You helped a pet rat have babies?"

He nodded. "It was Lanea's pet. First litter, and she couldn't seem to get it all done by herself. Lanea was scared. I was there, so I helped her." The simplicity of his words showed more about how much he cared for his cousin than anything else he could have said. "Ten little pink pups and one tired momma rat made it just fine."

Despite the circumstances under which we met, I had to admit, Runner was a good man. I said a little prayer for him to find peace as we brought Sennit to justice.

CHAPTER 17

Crank:

Watching that kid come into the world was a serious mind-fuck. Earlier, I realized I wanted to put my baby in Sarah's belly, but now I knew what the coming out part entailed, I wasn't so sure. Could I watch her go through that? Or worse, take the risk of not being there for her when the time came? I sat out there on the porch, lost in thought, for a long time before Runner came out to join me.

"You doing okay, man? That shit was intense."

I tossed my cigarette butt over the porch rail. "Yeah, I never really thought about it before, you know? Ol' ladies get knocked up, kids come out, all's right with the fucking world."

"At least neither one of us passed out." He laughed a little. "Two Case hit the floor like a brick when his kid came out."

"Shit, I can see that fucking happening to me." Nothing much bothered me usually, whether it was moving a corpse or torturing a fucker, but that right there was entirely fucking in a different world.

Sarah came out on the porch before I could think any more about it. "Do you think we could go over to the hospital? Chancey left so fast, she didn't get a chance to take anything with her. She'll want some clothes and stuff."

Made sense. "Yeah, okay."

Runner straightened in his chair. "Actually, if you get

the stuff together, I can take it to her. I was planning to stop by anyway."

Sarah lifted an eyebrow just a little, but didn't argue. "Sure. It'll only take me a few minutes." She disappeared back inside.

"Thanks. I have to admit I was kind of dreading going over there." The thought of seeing Chancey again so soon after watching her push that kid out of her body got to me.

"No problem. I'd be passing right by there anyway."

I figured it was more than that, but left it alone. Sarah came back in less than fifteen minutes with a small overnight bag. "I think I got everything. She had a bag ready, so I just added her phone, keys, and purse."

Runner accepted the bag and stood. "If she needs anything else, I can take care of it. It'll give me something to think about instead of what Lanea is doing."

"Wondered how you were going to handle that. It won't be easy to stay back."

"No, it won't. This way I can hang back a little for now." He pulled his phone out and tapped out a text. "Okay, my ride is on the way. I'll head on out to the road, and see you in a couple days."

Sarah sat down with me as he left. "What next?"

"We pack up and head back." I wished we could stay there a while longer, in between, and enjoy getting to know each other better. "When we have this all wrapped up, I'd like to come back, though."

She smiled and raised a hand to brush my hair back out of my eyes. "I would too." The quick hard kiss caught me by surprise, and she drew back before I could deepen it. "I'll go get our stuff packed. If it's okay, I want to clean the room so Chancey doesn't have to do it when she gets home."

Pride rolled through me again. My woman took care of her friends. That kind of loyalty was a perfect quality in an ol' lady. "I'll help. She'll be away a few days, right?"

"I think it's usually three days, but I don't know if that's for the baby or the mother, or both. I can't imagine how she'll be able to walk for at least a week after that." Her laughter spilled over, making me grin.

"Shit, I know. And I sure as fuck can't figure out why anybody would do that more than once." I stood and pulled her under my arm. Time for a confession. "When we're fucking, I want more than anything to put my kid in your belly. Watching you grow our baby would be fucking incredible. But I never really thought much about how the kid gets out of there. I don't know how I could ask you to go through that."

Sarah went still against my side when I mentioned my little fantasy, and when I stopped talking, she didn't move. "You would want a baby with me?" Why did she sound like that was so far-fetched?

Had she not considered a future with me? "I want everything with you. A home. Kids. Getting old together." My chest hurt with the tension. "But I get it. I'm not exactly the kind of man a woman like you wants to spend her future with." Fuck. Could I just walk away and let her live her life?

A sudden tremor shook her. "I thought you wouldn't want anything more than a fling with me, or whatever they call it." She turned, facing me. "Crank, you live a different kind of life than me. Women throw themselves at you. I'm ashamed that I did it, too."

I sat back down and pulled her into my lap. "You're right. My life is very different. I fucking make my own rules, and that comes with risks. I, and the Hell Raiders, don't give much of a flying fuck about the law, but we have...I guess you'd call it a code. We hold each other to a standard, and while we know the rest of the world sees it differently, we feel like there are some things so basic they cross all lines of society."

"You have a code? Like that old Code of the West thing?" She sounded surprised.

"I don't know anything about that. But no Hell Raider will hurt a kid, or stand by and watch one be abused. We don't beat on our women. We bend over backwards not to harm innocents in our business." Putting it into words strained my abilities. "We'll fight like a cornered wolf if the need comes, but we don't pull civilians into our shit."

She looked a little shocked by that, but nodded her head. "You have honor."

"Some people would call it that. To us, it's just how we are."

"And what about all the women? I'm not stupid. You're sexy as sin, and so are the other Hell Raiders I've seen. I know how women act around men like you. They all want your attention." She'd obviously been thinking about this.

"Yeah, there are women. Sometimes a lot of them." I leaned down to brush my lips over her forehead. "The outlaw life has been made to look fun to a whole bunch of people who watch it on TV. And, fuck, it's always held a strong attraction to certain women. Back home, if we have an open party, a lot of chicks show up, hoping for a little taste of the wild side. And there's the club girls. They're not ol' ladies, and some are available whenever a Brother is lonely. They're also under Club protection." Fuck, there was so much to explain.

"That's what I mean. I can't compete with that, and I can't share. To me, that would be cheating, and it goes against everything I believe." The seriousness of her voice backed up her fears.

"Sarah, I'm no saint. I haven't lived a celibate life. I've fucked a *lot* of chicks. But I don't cheat. If I'm with a woman, I'm there a hundred percent." I tipped her chin up to make sure she could see what I was saying. "I'm with you Sarah. You're my woman. I won't allow another man to touch you. And I expect that same kind of possessiveness from you. If you let some bitch rub up all over me at a party, to me, it would say you didn't care enough to tell her to back the fuck off."

The way her eyes widened told me I'd reached her. "But I thought..."

"You thought I would continue to fuck any chick that offered?"

She nodded and lowered her gaze. Yeah, that's what she fucking thought.

"I don't know, I'm sure some bastards do that. That's not me. When I make a commitment, I keep it." I couldn't think of a clearer way to say it.

"Are we...committed? Together?"

"I hope like fuck we are. I want a future with you, even if you do deserve better than me. I'm a selfish bastard for that, I guess. But I can't be enough of a good guy to just fucking let you go." The words surprised me a little. I'd been feeling it, thinking it, but had no intention of saying it yet.

Sarah slipped her arms around me and hugged me tight. "Good."

Something inside me broke. She wanted me, and all that meant. I couldn't even begin to fucking process that. It had to wait until I had a little time to put it all together. I leaned down to kiss her. "Let's go get our shit packed and clean up our mess. We got people waiting for us." It was the coward's way out, but at the moment, I didn't give a fuck. Besides, it was true.

It took a little longer to pack our shit than I expected.

Sarah wasn't the kind of girl to travel with one change of clothes and a little makeup. I watched with something like amazement as she folded clothes, separated out what she'd already worn, and packed everything. I'd never known a chick to be so particular over things like that.

Cleaning up turned into a more involved prospect than I figured, too. Not only did Sarah insist on stripping the bed, she put on fresh sheets and stuff. Then it was time for the bathroom. It got a thorough cleaning, and fresh towels. And then the floors. By the time we finished, I felt like I needed an apron and a housekeeping cart. But it made Sarah happy to do something for her friend, so I didn't mind.

Finally, we started back to Randolph as night fell. Wary of what we might be rolling into, I stopped long enough to call ahead and check in with Fergus' man, and double-check my weapons. I'd rather keep Sarah somewhere safe while I went after Sennit, but without my Brothers here, I couldn't trust anyone to truly look out for her. That kind of vulnerability didn't sit well with me.

Outside town, we met up with one of the Walkers and switched our vehicle for another big SUV, just another make, model and color. The precaution against Sennit's men realizing we were back in town wouldn't fool anyone who looked too closely, but maybe it would give us a little time.

Checking in at the rundown little motel Fergus and I chose to use as a sort of base only took a few minutes. Sarah looked around the little room like it was something stuck on the bottom of her shoe. Shame rolled through me. She'd never been in a place like that, and I didn't like being the one to bring her to it. She deserved nothing but the best. Right fucking then, I knew I would do anything I could to make sure she had the best life had to offer.

CHAPTER 18

Sarah:

The room stank. The dim light beside the bed revealed a carpet crusted with filth, concealing both the color and the nap. Grime hid the dingy wallpaper near the door, and at the corner leading to the bathroom. The dark print of the bedspread blended with several questionable looking spots.

Through my work, I had seen appalling living conditions, gone into homes crawling with cockroaches and other vermin, and conducted investigations in places filled with unimaginable filth. But this was different. I was expected to eat and sleep here, in this little patch of unsanitary hell. Could I actually do it? I wasn't so sure. The door closed with a thud, startling me, and I turned to face Crank, ready to run.

He looked around with the same distaste I felt. "This was a mistake. We'll find something else." Someone tapped at the door before he could open it. He raised one finger to gesture for me to stay silent, and quickly stepped outside.

My pulse hammered in my head while I waited. Was something wrong? Had Sennit figured out what we were doing?

Crank came back in after just a moment, followed by another man. "Sarah, this is Two Case, one of the guys keeping an eye on Lanea."

The man gave a sort of half nod in my direction.

"Hi. Nice to meet you."

His eyes flickered toward me, but he stayed silent.

"Looks like I spoke too soon, Sarah. There's no other place to stay that's close enough. Lanea's at a foster home just across the street." Crank seemed more upset about it than I was.

I shrugged a little. "It's okay." I glanced around. "It's really not that bad." Yes, it was, but I had to try to convince myself.

"Shouldn't be for long. Two Case said Sennit is already sniffing around."

"Is the home a good one?" I went to the window and pulled the flimsy curtain aside to look out. I suddenly realized where we were. "Oh, no, it's not. I have tried to get those people out of the foster parent program for the longest time. But I never had anything really solid to go on."

Two Case nodded. "Yeah, they bad. Maybe you'll get the dirt to shut them down now."

"I hope so. I know there's more going on there than crowded conditions, but the children are always afraid to talk." I didn't blame them. The husband was a formidable person physically, and very stern. The wife seemed meek and quiet, and very clearly deferred to him on everything. Shutting them down seemed like a reasonable cause to stay in the nasty little motel for as long as it took.

"Any word on how it's going so far?" Crank pulled out a cigarette and lit it before offering the pack to Two Case, who declined. That smell, one I'd always detested, comforted me a little. My mind associated it with Crank, and Crank meant safety.

"Nothing unusual so far. They brought her in, the woman told her the rules and showed her to a bed. The man's not home yet. I expect if there's anything tonight, it'll be from him."

"Maybe one of the kids will talk to her. I know in some homes they warn newcomers about things that can get them into trouble." At least I hoped they would talk to Lanea.

Two Case nodded. "They might. Or she might be too Indian for them."

That hadn't occurred to me. "Will she be okay?"

"She's used to it. We all are. Plenty of people around here still believe the only good Indian is a dead one, or that we all belong in teepees on the rez." He gave an expressive shrug. "Just part of life."

Crank gave a little cough. "Any place around here good to eat?" Just like that, he shifted the conversation back to neutral territory. "I'm about starved."

Two Case grinned, showing startlingly white teeth. "Yeah, man, there's a little dairy bar thing about halfway down the block. Best damn cheeseburgers in the state. Tell them I sent you, and Julie will treat you right."

"Perfect. Sarah, you ready for a burger?"

"Most definitely. I should probably stay out of sight, though. If one of the children, or the parents, see me, they'll recognize me." I didn't need to follow the logic to see how that could endanger Lanea.

"You got a spare ball cap, Two Case?" Crank gave me a speculative look. "You don't normally wear jeans to work, right?"

"No, why?"

"They're not likely to recognize you dressed differently and with your hair covered, unless they get a close look at your face."

Two Case nodded. "He's right. Back in a minute." He left, and came back moments later, with a hat.

With Crank's help, I threaded my hair through the back

of the hat in a sort of pony tail. It felt weird to pull the brim down over my forehead.

Two Case opened the door. "That does it. No one will know you unless they get close." He offered a hand to Crank, who accepted. "I'm gonna get back over here and see if there's anything new. And I'll see what I can do about the room."

The thin disguise left me feeling incredibly vulnerable as we left the room. I kept my head down, and stayed close to Crank. The walk to the dairy bar seemed to take forever, but finally, we arrived without anyone questioning me. Relief flushed my face with heat.

Crank gave the girl at the counter our order, then led me to a booth at the back. He leaned close. "Stop trying to hide like you're on the FBI's most wanted list, or some shit. Just be normal and no one will question it."

He was right, of course. I tried to stop acting like a fugitive. The food came and we ate without talking, listening to the ebb and flow of conversation around us. By the time we finished, I definitely felt better. I sat back, trying to decide if I could finish the last half of my chocolate shake.

"Miss Channing? Is that you?" The voice sent ice water rolling down my spine. "Who's your friend? We've missed you at work." Jared Sennit strolled over to our table.

I must have gone white as a sheet, because Crank squeezed my hand. "Mr. Sennit. What a surprise." My brain stuttered to a standstill. Our whole plan was blown now. We would never get another chance at making this right.

Crank stood and offered Sennit a hand. I couldn't help but swell with pride at the way Crank towered over him, all muscle and aggression. "You must be Sarah's boss. Have a seat. I'm James Harrison." He took Sennit's hand, despite Sennit holding back.

"I really don't have the time. I was just surprised to see Miss Channing here." Sennit moved back, trying to get out of Crank's space.

Crank followed. "No, really, I insist." He pulled a chair over from a nearby table. "Sit."

Clearly reluctant, Sennit sat. "I wouldn't want to intrude."

"Oh, but you're not. I intended to come see you at your office later. You saved me the trip." Crank's bloodthirsty grin made Fergus seem harmless.

Sennit swallowed hard. "What business could you have at my office?" Another man putting him on the spot definitely shook him.

"Several things, actually. Are you aware someone broke into Sarah's apartment?"

Sennit shook his head. "No, I hadn't heard. Who would do that? Was anything taken?" He glanced my way.

I started to answer, but Crank interrupted. "Nothing important. But someone claiming to be you also stopped by her parents' house, and said you were having a relationship with her."

"Why would someone do that?" He seemed more sure of himself now.

"I'm not sure, but I'm going to find out. On both accounts. Sarah is my fiancé, and I won't have anyone hurting her, or claiming her." He gave that bloodthirsty grin again. "Where I'm from, that's a killing offense, and I won't hesitate."

Sennit smiled. "Where are you from, Mr. Harrison, was it?"

Crank's eyes went cold and he pulled his jacket aside a little to show the handle of gun tucked into his waistband. "I'm from where-the-fuck-ever I want to be. I make my own laws, and enforce them with blood."

The laughter sounded forced, and Sennit definitely turned a shade or two paler than normal. "Very convincing, Mr. Harrison." He turned toward me. "Miss Channing, I never took you for the sort who would take up with a thug."

Crank leaned in close. "A thug is just a pussy putting on airs, Mr. Sennit. I promise you, I don't make empty threats, and I don't front." He leaned back. "Oh, hey, Sennit, how's that chick who lived down the street from your folks when you were in high school? What was her name? Fuck, I can't remember it now. You know the one, she got raped and beaten half to death. You must have been, what, sixteen?"

Sennit's face went red. "Miss Channing, I'll expect to see you at work tomorrow. I'm afraid I don't have time for these games." He stood.

"No, she won't be at work until I get this shit sorted out." Crank stood with him, once more crowding into his personal space.

Sennit glared at him for a moment, then turned and stalked away.

Finally, I could breathe. "Oh my God! He knows! We have to get her out of there."

Crank sat down and took my hands in his. "Look at me, Sarah." When I complied, he continued. "He doesn't know fuck. That's why I pushed him. He'll be looking at me, trying to figure out my next move, and not focusing on details that seem normal."

"But he knows we know about him."

"He knew that already. But he thinks he's smarter, so there's no way we could get anything on him. And now, he's more concerned I'll bust the windows out of his car than anything else." He grinned. "And I might do that, just for the hell of it."

I couldn't really follow his logic. "So you let him think you're just some petty criminal?"

"Exactly. He'll be worried for his personal safety, just in case I decide to beat the piss out of him. But he'll disregard me as any other kind of threat, and he'll continue business as usual." He reached over to brush a thumb over my lip. "That's what we want, Sarah. He'll be too busy watching for me to jump out at him from a dark alley that he won't consider I might be watching for something else."

"Okay. I think." Something else he had said suddenly lodged in my mind. "Why did you tell him that I'm your fiancé?" We hadn't discussed marriage, or anything more than a nebulous sort of future.

"Because, you're mine, Sarah." His eyes went dark and serious. "I'm not good enough for you, and not at all the kind of man you should be with, but I'm not strong enough to give you up, either."

My heart pounded against my ribs with bruising force. "Are you sure that's what you want?"

His eyes darkened a little. "I'm very fucking sure. I know you have doubts, and I'll give you time to get used to the idea. But it's going to happen, Sarah." He smiled, and started to say something else, but his phone buzzed an interruption. "Fuck."

He answered the call. "Yeah." After a short pause he nodded. "On our way." The phone disappeared back into his pocket. "We have to go. The boys got something."

When he stood and offered a hand to assist me in a gesture as natural as his coarse language, my heart melted a little more. As rough as he could be at times, his natural inclinations seemed to be those of a gentleman. How had a man raised as he had been learned things like that? It was just one more question to the puzzle Crank presented. One I could spend a lifetime solving.

CHAPTER 19

Crank:

I took the long way back to the motel, just in case Sennit had enough brains to watch. Anyone watching for us would have to prowl through the fucking place in a deliberate search to find us. By concentrating on concealment, I managed to avoid thinking about what I'd said to Sarah at the diner.

Two Case met us at the door of the room he and the others had set up as a sort of surveillance station. "Took you long enough."

"Sennit spotted us at the diner." I gave him a summary of that bullshit.

"Good, you laid a false trail." He gestured us over to a table where a laptop sat open. "One of the kids talked to Lanea. You should hear it."

I took a seat in the surprising clean chair, and pulled Sarah to sit on my lap. "Okay."

He clicked something on the screen, and voices filled the room. I recognized Lanea's voice immediately.

"This place doesn't seem as bad as I expected. I need to watch out for anything?"

A female laughed. "Girl, you ain't got a clue. The man picks one of us for a blowjob, or more, every night. The woman knows, and doesn't care."

"Nobody tells the caseworker?"

Another laugh. "Hell no. And you won't either, if you

know what's good for you."

"Why?"

"For one, we don't get dinner until he gets off. So whoever gets picked has to do a good job. For two, if you tell the caseworker, then the boss caseworker gets involved. He's a lot worse than giving a blowjob a couple times a week."

"What's he do?"

"Girl, he'll peddle your ass on the street. Or sell you to rich old dudes that can't get off without leaving bruises, or worse. So you give the blowjobs when he picks you, and keep your mouth shut the rest of the time. Mr. Sennit will be around to see you soon. He always comes see the new kids. And you'll do whatever he tells you, and you won't say a word about what happens here. If you do, the shit comes down on all of us, and we ain't going to be very happy with you."

A moment of silence. "What will this Mr. Sennit want from me?"

"He likes to be the first to fuck the new kids. The old man won't take more than a blowjob from you until he gives the go-ahead. You had your cherry popped?"

Something rustled, like fabric. "No. That's why I'm here. My mom got remarried, and her old man wanted me, but I got out first. Mom was glad to be rid of me, so she let me just stay with her sister. My aunt was always high on something, and social services got called eventually."

The other girl made a noise. "Well, you better not tell Mr. Sennit that. A virgin brings a high price. He'll auction your cherry off. Better just let him do it and not say a word."

"No. If I wanted to just give it away, I'd have let my mom's old man do it."

More rustling, and someone grunted. "Bitch, you listen. You ain't got no choice. The kinda mens he'll sell you to? They *ruin bitches. I seen girls they had, couldn't walk or sit up for weeks. One girl died, bled to death after the man shoved something in her and tore her insides all up. Mr. Sennit is scum, but he just a straight fuck."*

A choking sound. "Oh." More rustling. "How does he get by with it? I seen on the news where they put a kid in jail for fucking his underage girlfriend. This gotta be way more against the law."

The other girl gave a rough laugh. "Yeah, it is. But that was just a kid, not a growed man who knows how to cover his tracks, and how to make people say what he want. They say some girl tried to report Mr. Sennit. She turned up dead, right in her bed, strangled during the night. Two other kids in the house took the fall for it. After that, nobody say a fucking word."

A door slammed in the background, then another female voice. "Emma, you filling the new girl in on how things work here?"

"Yes, Mrs. Baker. She understands the rules now."

"Very good. The two of you come out here and get dinner started. Mr. Baker will be home soon."

Two Case click the audio off. "Rest of it's just normal shit, them cooking food and talking about school."

Sarah sat on my lap, tense and pale, with her hands over her mouth. I pulled her back against me. "It's okay, Sarah. This is what we need."

"So we can get her out now?"

Fuck. I shook my head. "No, we need more than just one girl talking scary shit to a new girl."

Two Case nodded. "Yeah, talking shit like that to scare the piss out of the new kid is common. We need it from Sennit. And we want the rest of his cronies, too."

Sarah looked sick. "I don't know if I can stand listening

to this, Crank. To think, I put children where this predator could get to them. I'm as much to blame as he is." A big tear rolled down her cheek.

"First of all, Sarah, you had no idea what he was doing, right?"

She nodded, and another tear spilled over.

"You took kids out of bad situations and tried to make them safe, right?"

"Yes, but I should have seen the signs. Should have paid more attention." She turned into my chest. "I can't believe this is happening, and that I didn't see it."

"There are other caseworkers working with Sennit, right? Been there longer than you?"

She nodded with a sob.

"Did they know?"

She shook her head.

"No, because he was good at covering his tracks. Sarah, Sennit is a life-long sexual predator. He learned to keep his shit covered long ago, and he's good at it. For some reason, that one girl, out of dozens, maybe hundreds, of his victims, chose to talk to you. You didn't shrug it off and tell him, like you could have. You poked around, put yourself in danger. It's time to stop fucking with your own head and help us bring this bastard down."

She stayed silent, so I just rubbed her back, trying to soothe her.

Two Case stood up. "Hey, man, I had your stuff moved to another room. That shithole they put you in is supposed to be for the hourly-rate customers."

"Kinda figured that, but I didn't know if they had anything better."

"Yeah, the rooms up front are for the whores and

junkies. Better rooms are in the back." He passed me a key. "Two fifteen. Ain't no second floor, but I guess they wanted the place to sound bigger or something. I'm in two sixteen."

"Thanks, man, appreciate it." I tucked Sarah's hair back. "Come on, darlin', we'll go get settled in." When she stood, I followed, and accepted Two Case's hand. "Let me know when you need me on the listening schedule." I dreaded that particular duty, but I would do my part.

"I will. We should have it covered unless something comes up."

We found the new room easily, not far from where I'd parked the car earlier. Sarah held her breath a little as I unlocked the door, then sighed with relief when she stepped inside with me. As clean as any of the big chain hotels, probably cleaner, the room had plenty of light, and smelled of disinfectant and air freshener.

"Thank God. I was afraid of that other room." She sank onto the bed, looking around.

"Yeah, I have to admit, I was too. I've slept in a few rat holes, but that was a whole new level of nasty even for me." Who knew what the fuck infested the other room. I was glad we didn't have to find out.

"I wonder why they set up the listening stuff in one of those rooms?" Her voice now held curiosity, rather the grief and dread from earlier.

"Reception, probably. The closer the transmission source is, the clearer the audio comes in." She didn't need to know they wanted to be physically closer to Lanea, too, in case something went wrong and she needed backup fast. I hadn't missed the weapons within easy reach in the room. They were ready to roll if she needed them.

"Oh. That makes sense. I guess having a whole building

in between might interfere with the signal or something."

"Probably." I checked my bag, just to be on the safe side, and found everything as I'd left it. The mini-fridge sat on the dresser, beside the TV, and I found it stocked with beer, water, and a few soft drinks. "Two Case has been busy." I took out a beer, and offered Sarah a water.

"He did that?"

"Yeah. I'll get one of them to bring in some food in the morning. That way, we don't have to go out unless we want Sennit to see us."

"Why would we want that?"

I shrugged. "Just to rattle his fucking cage a little. Keep him off balance." I drained the rest of my beer and tossed the can. The way Sarah sat there on that bed, all unsure of herself, pushed my buttons and my dick swelled uncomfortably in my jeans. "You want to get your shower first? Because if you keep sitting there, I'm going to fuck you before you have a chance to."

Her eyes widened with surprise and she stood quickly. "Yes. A hot shower sounds like a good idea." She grabbed her bag and darted for the bathroom.

"Hey, Sarah."

She turned to look at me just before she closed the door. "Yes?"

"Leave the door unlocked."

Her lips parted. "Okay." She closed the door softly.

I tormented myself, imagining her getting undressed, seeing every inch of skin as it was revealed, until the water came on. My dick throbbed, begging me to go through that door and join her.

No.

She needed some time.

My dick cursed me, but I turned the TV on, instead of following orders. Searching through the channels, I found something that passed for local news. I even tried to pay attention to it, but nothing registered.

Fifteen minutes. I could live fifteen minutes before I opened that door and got in the shower with her. The image of water cascading down Sarah's body cut the time. Ten minutes.

I gave up at seven, and stripped out of my clothes, dropping them on the floor. At eight minutes, I stepped into the cloud of steam that filled the bathroom. The textured glass of the shower doors only hinted at the beauty beyond. I made it until nine minutes before I opened that door and stepped inside with her.

CHAPTER 20

Crank:

She had her back to me, rinsing shampoo from her hair. Fucking irresistible. Wary of startling her, I spoke before touching her. "Hey darlin', need someone to wash your back?"

"Mmm, only if he's tall, dark, and sexy as sin."

No further invitation needed, I grabbed her bottle of shower gel, dumped some in my hand and lathered it up. I started with her back, stroking all that silky skin, then pulled her against me to reach her front. Her tits filled my hands, built just for me.

A soft moan escaped her as she let her head drop back on my shoulder when I thumbed her nipples. A light pinch earned me her ass thrust back against my hard-on. Fuck, I might die before I could get inside her.

I moved us back until my shoulders touched the end of the shower wall, then let one hand leave her tit and slide down. A light brush of my fingers over her pussy, and she thrust back harder. She easily spread her legs in response to my knee between hers.

"Bend over, baby, put your hands on the wall." The words nearly choked me. I dipped a finger between her folds and brushed over her clit, and she responded immediately, allowing me to line my dick up to her opening.

I buried my cock in her, and she met me halfway. We balanced there, basically on imagination, driving together, wet slapping sounds filling the air when our bodies met. My brain refused to register a goddamn thing, except the way her pussy gripped my cock, and the way my balls tightened.

Then suddenly all that wet heat rippled around me, squeezing, as she cried out. I locked inside her, helpless, coming until my balls turned inside out.

Keeping us upright turned into a real struggle as I returned to earth, and I finally had to lean against the side of the shower. How the fuck did she keep doing that to me? Every time I intended to play a little, and last long enough to make sure she thoroughly enjoyed it, her tight pussy clamped down and I lost it like a damn teenager.

Finally, able to stand somewhat steadily, I withdrew from her and helped her rinse off. That slick body tempted me to start again, even though my dick refused to show any signs of life. Eventually, I let her go reluctantly, so she could get dried off. I took three whole minutes to deal with the condom and wash up, then followed her.

She smiled up at me from where she sat on the side of the bed, toweling her hair dry. "You are just full of surprises."

"I am?" I searched my memory.

She nodded. "You know more delicious ways to have sex than any man on earth."

The laugh came out before I could stop it. "Darlin', you have no idea. That's okay, though. I'll happily spend the rest of my life fucking educating you." The thought that she lacked experience pleased me. I leaned in to let my mouth trail over her exposed neck.

A little shiver raced over her. "I'll just bet you will." Her head tipped back as her soft laughter filled the room.

I froze. That sexy, satisfied gleam in her eyes. I put that there. She fucking destroyed me with that look. Anything she wanted, I would do whatever it fucking took to put the same expression on her face again.

Shit. I needed some fucking distance. Nobody ever had that kind of power over me. With the way my life went, I couldn't afford it. The criminal in me drew away from her. "I'm going go over and see if Two Case has anything new. Be back in a few minutes." And I fucking bolted for my jeans.

"Okay. I think I'll go on to bed. It's been a long day."

"Yeah, it has. I'll be quiet when I come back in." I tugged my boots on, and pulled my t-shirt over my head. I leaned down to steal another kiss. "You keep that gun handy, yeah? Just in case."

She smiled and touched my jaw. "I'll be fine."

I turned away before I could confirm a tear glistened on her lashes. All the way over to the other room, I fucking cursed myself for walking out on her like that. Everything in me said go back, and hold her close, and never let go. Too fucking many people already knew she was important to me. It put her at risk. The best thing for her would be for me to go grab a pack of smokes and get the fuck up out of town.

Fergus and his boys were onto Sennit now, and they would hunt him down like a dog, so she would be safe from him. Sarah could go back to her nice small-town life, and get the kind of husband who worked regular hours, was home for dinner every night, brought her flowers on her birthday, took her out for date night once a week, and fucked her twice a week. My mind seized up on that last part. The thought of any other man touching her, ever, rocked me with a need for violent revenge.

I tapped at the door and stood clear so Two Case could see me easily. He swung the door open and signaled me to stay quiet. Lanea's voice filled the room on the audio playback from the laptop.

"...never done that before. I don't know how."

A man grunted. "Then it's time you learn. You just suck on it."

"But...it's gross. I'll get sick." She sounded timid, frightened.

"Not if you know what's good for you." The man's impatience came clearly through the speakers. "Now get down on your knees and get busy. Your boyfriend will thank me for teaching you."

Lanea's panicked-sounding breathing raised my hackles. When we started this, I assumed she was no shy virgin, but if she wasn't truly terrified, she was doing a damn good job acting.

The muffled whimpers, followed by retching, sent a chill down my spine. "I-I can't—"

"You will. They all do. Now quit playing."

She cried out. "Don't pull my hair!"

"Girl, shut up and suck, or I'll do a hell of a lot more." The fucker had no intentions of stopping.

A full ten minutes of choked sobs, punctuated by the man's groans of appreciation held us all in rigid fury.

Every shred of my instincts demanded I go snatch Lanea away from that monster and show him a little Hell Fire. I made a mental note to make sure and explain that principle to Fergus and his boys, and get them in on the party. Because that fucker was done raping kids.

I growled as the man shouted when he came, and Lanea gagged. "Two Case, is she that good an actress? Or has she really never done this stuff before?"

He shrugged and turned the audio down, maintaining that unreadable expression. "Don't know for sure, but I don't think she's acting. Girl is a warrior, always training, but even though she talks tough, she's never shown much interest in males. Females either, for that matter."

"Fuckkk. I wouldn't have agreed to her going in if I'd known that, and I know Sarah wouldn't have." I slammed a fist into the flimsy paneling on the wall, and was rewarded with a satisfying splintering noise.

"Don't break the wall, motherfucker. Calm down. Lanea is not stupid. She knew exactly what was going to happen. She chose to go ahead anyway, because this is about family honor to her. She loves Runner, and she knows what happened to him. For a long time, she's the only one he talked to. She's been waiting to avenge him, and the family, for years." He tossed me a beer from the fridge and cracked one open for himself.

The first swallow did nothing to lessen my fury. "I don't care, man. She can't let herself be raped, repeatedly, just to put that fucker in jail. Pull her out. We find another way."

Two Case grinned. "Sennit, and that scum over there, won't go to jail. Lanea will deliver that justice."

"What kind of justice?"

"She's a wizard with blades. For every piece of her they take, she'll take a hundred pieces of them."

"She doesn't have to let them rape her to do that." The thought of Lanea cutting the bastards to bits pleased me, but her going through so much to justify it absolutely gutted me. "They already deserve it."

"Yes they do. But your woman needs solid evidence to turn over to the FBI, or whoever, to get this whole mess wrapped up. Lanea only wants Sennit, and whoever hurts her during this."

As much as I wanted to, I really couldn't argue with the logic. It might sicken me, but Lanea was a grown woman, and this was her choice. "One condition. I have a little of my own justice I want to give Sennit."

"You'll get your chance before she kills him."

"Good." I lit a smoke, which reminded me of why I should leave, and not come back. "Got a question for you. This is going forward, right? Whether I'm around or not?"

"It can't be stopped. Why? You taking your woman and leaving?"

"Not taking her. You'll keep her safe from Sennit until he's gone?" My lungs went tight, reminding me to fucking breathe.

"How you going to show him justice if you leave?"

"I'll stick around long enough for that. Just might not always be visible." Gut-churning fear threatened to consume me. Could I really walk away? Could I live without her?

Two Case shook his head. "She'll be safe. But, no offense, man, you're making a massive mistake. She's a good woman."

I swallowed hard, trying to keep from emptying my stomach right there on the floor. "Yeah, she is. That's the point. Good women don't make it long in the MC life. It's too much for them. And I can't leave it behind."

"The women you Raiders pick must be a different breed then. Out here, good women stand by their man, no matter what. You have to treat them right, shield them a little from the worst parts. But you owe it to her to let her decide."

So maybe he was right. That didn't change things, though. All the way back to the room, I thought about it. What would Sarah think of me when she learned the kinds of things I actually did? Love or respect sure as fuck wouldn't be at the top of her list. I'd rather her hate me for leaving than for the way I lived.

CHAPTER 21

Sarah:

I lay there for a long time after he left, trying to hold the tears at bay. I felt it, as clearly as if he slapped me. One moment he was warm, close, loving, and the next, a door slammed closed and he was suddenly distant. The connection disappeared. Whatever happened, I missed him.

Eventually I gave up the battle and let the sobs come. Had I lost him, before I even really had him? Instinct told me yes. My tears stopped after a time, and I stared at the ceiling, searching for some solution in the shadows the light from the window cast over the irregularities of the paint.

A faint sound at the door brought me back to reality in a flash. The scent of his cigarette preceded him into the room. "I was starting to think you'd gotten lost."

"Shit, sorry. I didn't mean to wake you." He fiddled with the door for a moment.

"You didn't." I sat up in bed. "I couldn't sleep."

The tip of his cigarette glowed. "No fucking wonder. Lot going on lately."

"That's putting it mildly." He clearly had no intention of talking about exactly what kept me awake. And I was pretty sure he knew.

"I'm gonna grab a shower. Try to get some rest." And just like that, he ended the conversation, closing the bathroom door firmly behind him.

My tears threatened to start again, but I kept taking deep breaths, holding them back. He had a lot on his mind, too, unless he made a habit of pretending to fall in love with women, then leaving. Somehow, I didn't think he was the type for that.

I played everything back in my head, from the time we arrived here. He had seemed so intense about his feelings for me, so certain. And then, after we made love in the shower, just all of a sudden, he pulled back. It made no sense. This whole time, he pressed me, with his talk about a future, and spending the rest of his life with me. Without that, thoughts of a real future with him probably would never have taken root in my mind. Of course, I would have dreamed of it, but I'd have known it couldn't happen. We were from two different worlds. So what happened to change it all?

Sleep still refused to come by the time he turned the shower off. A few moments later, he came out, and his scent hit me like a wave of pleasure. When had I come to associate the smell of whatever soap he used with the ecstasy he could give me? A glimpse of his bare chest took my breath away, and I allowed my gaze to go lower, only to stop cold. He always came to bed nude, but this time, he wore a pair a baggy shorts.

The lump formed in my throat immediately, and threatened to choke me. He had a very clear way of making things known. It was over. For him, at least. My chest wanted to crack into pieces as he climbed into bed and lay carefully on his side, rather than folding me into his arms like he always did. Over.

For the longest time, I watched him, as his breathing evened out and his body relaxed into sleep. The questions ran through my mind in an endless stream. What happened? Had I done something wrong? Why did he even come back if he wanted to end things with me? I almost thought that would have been more merciful. This change in him really hurt.

At some point, I dozed off, but a sleepless night would have been better than the pain-filled dreams that chased me. I woke slowly, warm and secure with the heat of Crank's erection pressing against my hip. A nightmare. That's all it was. A terrible dream.

Then he tensed, and carefully pulled away from me.

Not a dream. Real. My body ached with the absence of his touch.

In any other situation, I would have accepted things and gone away quietly. I wasn't the type to really speak out. When I called him, angry that he ignored me after he went home, was the first time I asserted myself that much, especially with a man. Something of his attitude must have rubbed off on me.

I sat up, not bothering to pull the sheet over my breasts, and turned to face him. "Crank, what's going on?"

He looked up at me, inscrutable expression giving away nothing. "What do you mean?"

"You. One minute you're talking about the future, then you can't get away from me fast enough. So what's going on? Did you decide you don't want to be tied down to one woman, after all? Or did I do or say something wrong?"

For a fleeting second, something that looked like pain crossed his face, then it was gone, replaced by a frown. "I don't know what you're talking about." He got up with an abrupt movement, and turned to face me, hands at his sides. "This is me, Sarah. Nothing fancy. Nothing sentimental. I'm not an easy man to get along with." He made a noise that sounded like a smothered groan, and disappeared into the bathroom. When he came out, he was fully dressed. "I'm going to see if they have anything new yet." The door didn't slam behind him, but it made a firm point. He considered the subject closed.

Pain evaporated, replaced by anger. If he thought I was going to make this easy for him, he'd better think again. Where did he get off, thinking he could dangle forever in front of a girl like that, and then just snatch it back?

I started with a long shower, and took extra care with my hair and makeup. The limited wardrobe I'd managed to bring along made things a little more difficult. In the end, I ended up choosing a pair of snug jeans, ones I normally wouldn't wear for anything more than hanging around the house. I topped it off with a tank top that belonged under another top, but it showed the upper curves of my breasts, and I knew how much Crank liked those.

The woman who stared back at me from the mirror was a stranger, determined, sexy, and ready to fight for what she wanted. Where on earth did she come from? Doubt assailed me for a moment, but I took a deep breath, and turned to the door. No turning back.

Panic struck when I knocked on the door of the room where Two Case and the others set up their listening post. Would he even be there? If not, I could be in a lot of trouble. I didn't know those men.

Then the door opened, and it was too late for regrets. Two Case's eyes widened, and he gave a low whistle. "Well, good morning to you, too. Come in."

I stepped inside the room, trying not to look too anxious as I looked around for Crank, and didn't spot him immediately.

"Your ol' man went up the street to snag us some real coffee." Two Case grinned. "You got that boy wrapped pretty tight." He glanced at the other man in the room, seated before a laptop attached to a bunch of equipment, spread over the small table. "This here is Gator, and no, not because he's Cajun, or any shit like that."

I gave a careful smile. "Hi, Gator." I turned back to Two Case. "Am I supposed to ask why he's called that?"

His broad grin took me by surprise. "He fed his ol' lady's ex to a gator. Literally."

The blood drained from my face. "Oh."

The man with the murderous name glanced up from whatever he was doing. "Don't let him fool you. Bastard deserved it. Came after her while I was inside, and beat the hell out of her and our kid."

"Oh." How very eloquent of me. I was in so far over my head with these people, it was laughable, like something from a movie. "Was she happy when you did it?"

Gator nodded, pleased with the question. "She fed the gator the first finger while the fucker watched and screamed. He made her life a living hell for three years."

I gave a careful smile. When in Rome, right? "It's good he can't hurt her anymore, then."

Two Case pulled over a straight-back chair. "Here, have a seat. We'll catch you up on everything while Crank is gone."

I seemed to have passed some sort of test, judging by their demeanors. For the next twenty minutes, they told me about what happened to Lanea the night before, and how her morning was going. When I heard what that monster did to her, I retched in sympathy.

"We have to get her out of there."

Gator shook his head. "No, ma'am. She wouldn't want that. If she wants out, she'll let us know. In the old days, she would have been a warrior, fighting alongside the rest of us. This is how she can fight now, and she wants to do it. Needs to."

I nodded. It made a weird kind of sense to me.

Everything inside me might weep for what she was going through, and demand her rescue, but I could still equate her actions with my own. I had been reprimanded for taking risks at work several times. "Then we need to get it over with as quickly as possible."

Two Case gave me a look, as if reassessing my value, and finding himself surprised. "I have to be honest, Miss Channing, I didn't think you would take it this well."

"I'm not. But I know she has a job to do, and she wants to succeed. And call me Sarah."

He nodded as a knock came at the door. I stood while he went to open it, and tried to make myself small and invisible. Gator noticed, and gave me a wary look and a raised eyebrow, but said nothing.

Crank came in and placed two large bags carefully on the table. "Think I got everything." The way he looked at me betrayed his surprise to see me there, but he didn't say anything. He rummaged in one of the bags, pulling out creamer packs, then cups of coffee. "Sarah, I wasn't sure you'd be up, but I got you coffee, too."

At least he wasn't a total ass. "Thanks." I took the cup, added creamer, and stood back to wait.

He sat on the edge of one of the beds. "There's some donuts and shit in the other bag. Figured breakfast was in order."

"You figured right." Gator rose from his seat and went to search through the goodies. He chose a plain glazed donut, the offered the box to me. "Here, Sarah, I'm sure you're starving, too."

I couldn't help it. I gave him a sweet smile. "Aw, thank you, Gator. Such a gentleman." As I took the lemon-filled goodness from the box, I didn't miss Crank's scowl, but he stayed silent.

Emboldened, I sat on the bed beside him. "Did you enjoy your walk?"

He turned to me, his eyes immediately flaring with heat as they settled on my cleavage. "I did. It was a change of pace for me."

I took a big bite of my donut, careful to lick away some of the lemon filling. "Good. Time to think is always good."

He shifted a little, as if he were uncomfortable. "Not always." A careless sip of his coffee burned his tongue, bringing a hiss to his lips.

Taking advantage, I pressed close. "Are you okay?" I put my own cup safely on the little night table, and raised a finger to his lips.

His surprised breath puffed against my fingertip. "Yeah, I'll live." His lips clung to my skin a little.

Gator interrupted with a curse. "Sounds like Lanea will meet Sennit today." He clicked something on the computer, and hushed voices came through the speakers.

CHAPTER 22

Crank:

"You do exactly what he say. You don't, we all pay for it."

"I can't. Not after last night." Lanea sounded truly panicked.

"You ain't no better than the rest of us. We all have to do it. You do, too. So fuckin' deal." The other girl's anger threatened to spill over. *"He be here at nine, like for his regular visit. You go wit' him, and you do whatever he want. You make him real happy."*

The wire went quiet, as if the other girl left the room. Gator and Two Case sat there, looking as furious as I felt.

"Will we be able to get the others today?" Sarah's voice cut through the tension in the room.

"Doubt it." I shrugged. "He'll want to sample the goods before he offers her to paying customers." No way I could get that lucky and wrap this shit all up today, and be able to leave Sarah to live the life she was supposed to have.

She leaned against me, looking for reassurance, and I automatically slipped my arm around her before I realized it. "I hate for her to go through all this."

"Yeah, well, she went in knowing exactly what would happen." The words nearly choked me. "She's a grown woman, and this is her choice. Whatever happens is on her." Sounding like a total douche should get that starry-eyed look off Sarah's face.

Anger flared in her eyes. Bingo. "Knowing what will happen and living through it are two different things. And no, it isn't *on her*. It's on us. We came up with this brilliant plan. We put her in this position. So if she's hurt, it's our fault." She slid one hand along my forearm. "I know you hate this as much as I do, even if you are trying to act like it doesn't matter."

Well, fuck. I kept my voice down, rather than bring the other men into it. "Sarah, you're seeing good in me that doesn't fucking exist." That much was true, at least. I might try to fool myself sometimes by believing I lived by some moral code all my own, but when it came down to it, I was just a thug. Nothing more. And she deserved so much better.

"Crank, when you done ragging, I need a word with you." Gator's ominous tone raised my hackles. The man was hard to read, so I couldn't gauge what might be on his mind.

Partly to escape Sarah, I stood. "What's up?"

He lifted his chin. "Outside." He lit a smoke and went out the door.

I followed, ready to throw down if necessary. That ragging comment of his hadn't gone unnoticed. Inside the room, Two Case's voice rumbled, and I knew he was distracting Sarah from whatever Gator had on his mind.

Gator waited, leaning against the wall outside the door. I took a position not far away, but far enough, and leaned back a little, shoulders against the wall, and crossed my ankles. At least I didn't have to wait forever for him to get to the point.

Gator took a heavy drag from his cigarette. "Ain't my place to say, man, but I'm saying it anyways. You are fucking up, in a big way. You got a good woman there."

Annoyance surged. Who the fuck did he think he was? "You're right. It ain't your place to say. You ain't my momma.

So fuck off." I straightened, ready to go back inside.

"Hol' up, there, motherfucker. No, I ain't your momma, but I like Sarah. I'd hate like hell to see a good woman like her hurt for no good reason. So whatever mind fuck you got going on, get the fuck over it, brother. She don't deserve that shit." A heavy scowl and clenched fists guaranteed his seriousness.

"What the fuck do you know about her? You met her, what, ten minutes ago?" Another man defending my woman got under my skin. Bad.

He nodded. "Yeah, about that. Girl did not bat a lash when she heard how I got my name. She asked if it made my ol' lady happy. No disgust. No horror. She's the *only* citizen that has ever just accepted my reasons." The ash from his cigarette came dangerously close to hitting my boot, too close to a serious insult. "So it might not be my business, but I'm making it my business. What the fuck ever crawled up your ass, get your shit straight and treat her right. Don't treat that girl like a piece of shit junkie whore you're sick of having in your bed."

I sighed, suddenly exhausted. The fucker was right. "Better to hurt her feelings now, so she's nice and pissed at me when I leave."

"So you don't want nothing from her but a piece of ass while you're in town. That what's going on?"

Anger allowed the fucking words to slip out. "No. I want a life with her, want to marry her, put babies in her belly. But that can't happen." Fuck, I should just cut my own throat and get this shit over with.

"What, you got a wife back home?" He narrowed his eyes, more pissed than before.

"No. All you have to do is open your fucking eyes and look at her. She's a good girl. The kind that marries the high school football coach, organizes bake sales, and has a little white picket fence around the whole fucking thing." I swallowed hard. "And I'm a thug. Same as you. Can't drag her into the life, and can't leave it either."

Gator stared at me for a long time, and I nearly walked away. "You are the dumbest motherfucking individual I have ever met. She's strong. She's the kind of bitch you make shit work for, because you can't live without her. But that's okay, man. I know plenty of boys who'll gladly pick up the pieces once you're out of the picture." He lifted a hand in a mock salute and went back inside.

I stood there, pinned to the wall like a goddamn fly by his words. Then I shook it off. What the fuck did he know? Absolutely nothing, that's what. I went back inside, fuming, and ready for a fight.

Sarah looked up at me from where she still sat on the bed. "He's there."

My gut tightened. Why the fuck had I thought this was a good idea? God help me if I had to listen to that kid being raped. Yeah, she might be grown, technically, but her lack of experience made her a fucking kid. Jaw clenched with fury, I dropped into the empty chair. Couldn't go back to sitting next to Sarah. A soft word, or a touch, from her could undo all my resolve at this point.

"This is Lanea, our new girl." The male voice from last night echoed over the computer speakers. "Lanea, tell Mr. Sennit you're glad to meet him."

"H-h-hello, sir. Pleased to meet you." Fuck, she sounded terrified.

"Well, hello, Lanea. My, you are a pretty little thing. You must have boys sniffing after you all the time." Sennit sounded exactly like the slimeball he was.

"N-no, sir. I don't date." And just like that, she made

herself an irresistible target.

He practically drooled out loud. "Well, we can't have that. Girls your age need active social lives to be well-adjusted. Come on. I'll take you for a ride, and we can have lunch and get to know each other. It'll be good practice for you."

"I-I really need to go to school."

"Nonsense, girl." The other man needed to make sure she went along peacefully, it seemed. He would probably get paid better if she cooperated. "It's an excused absence, like I told you before. One day to get settled into your new home isn't going to be a problem."

"I d-don't—"

"I won't take no for an answer, Lanea. Now, go put on a nice dress. I'm sure some of the other girls here have something suitable. We're going to a nice place for lunch, so you have to look like you belong."

Everything went quiet again, and tension sat thick and heavy in the room. We waited, unable to speak, while Lanea prepared herself for Sennit. Only an occasional harsh breath, and the soft rustle of clothing indicated she was still there.

Why hadn't I just put a fucking bullet in Sennit's brain? It wouldn't have been the first time I killed some motherfucking piece of human scum. But no, I had to try that fucking white hat on for size, and try to get him and his buddies, and let the justice system punish them. Should have known better. I bit the inside of my jaw until blood flooded my mouth in my effort to keep the rage from escaping.

Reminding myself that Lanea wanted to do it this way, too, so she could get revenge for what happened to Runner only made things worse. If I hadn't come up with this stupid plan, she would never have known the difference, and Sennit would just be fucking gone.

"I'm shutting this shit down." I stood and started for the door.

"No." Two Case suddenly barred the way. "Lanea worried you would try to stop her once things started getting dirty. Gator and I have our orders. This goes forward as planned, unless she uses her safe word."

My field of vision narrowed as adrenaline flooded my system, preparing my body for a fight. "I don't give a fuck about your orders. It's done." I pushed him aside.

The distinctive sound of a gun being cocked came, followed closely by Sarah's little squeak of fear. "You best stop right there, Crank." Fucking Gator.

I turned slowly, ready to assess the risk and take my chances. "You prepared to kill me to make sure I don't interfere?"

The bastard gave a slow grin. "Nope." In a flash, he re-oriented the gun. On Sarah. "But I am prepared to kill her to make you stand down."

Motherfuck! That made no fucking sense at all. "You said you liked Sarah. Why would you hurt her? That's a fucking bitch move right there." I had to piss him off enough to get that gun turned back toward my head.

He raised his shoulder in a lazy half-shrug. "That's personal. This is business. You try to stop this before it's done, Sarah dies." The almost eager glitter in his eyes dared me to make a try. He might like Sarah, but a kill was a kill to him, and he liked it.

Sarah stayed silent through the exchange, proving her courage once more.

Another gun clicked behind me. "And just in case ol' Gator gets cold feet about his end of the job, I won't. Now you fucking stand down. It's gone too far now. If you stop it, Lanea won't get justice for what happened to her last night, or for Runner. She can't live with that."

I might have stood a chance of preventing Gator from harming Sarah, if it was just him. But with both of them against me, the odds of a win weren't worth the risk. I could wait. "Fine." I returned to the chair. The very moment I could ensure Sarah's safety, to hell with justice or whatever else they wanted to call it. I would put a stop to all of it. Except they were fucking right, and I fucking knew it.

CHAPTER 23

Sarah:

For a moment, the air felt too thick to get past the lump in my throat. No matter how much Crank tried to deny it, or for whatever reasons, he couldn't fool me. Beneath that tough exterior lay a good and decent man. The horror of what poor Lanea faced bothered him as much as it did me.

He sat with his arms folded over his chest, glaring at Gator and Two Case. Their actions a few minutes ago clearly angered him to the point of plotting revenge. While part of me wanted to warn them, the rest of me basked in the thrill of his willingness to surrender to protect me. The obvious blow to his pride spoke far louder than his sudden pulling away from me. No matter what he tried to prove, he still cared for me. I could live with that. For now.

I finally gave in to the uncomfortable tension in the room. "What do we do now?"

Two Case shook his head. "We wait. I have four of the boys following, so we'll know where he takes her. They'll be ready to move in if I give the word."

Crank made a sarcastic noise. "And when will that be? When the first pedophile has her spread eagled and bleeding? Or when the next one comes into the room?"

Gator frowned, but Two Case shook his head, and rather than speak, Gator turned back to the computer and put the headphones on. Two Case turned to face Crank squarely. "She's prepared for that if it is necessary."

Crank's growl rolled through the room and raised the hair on the back of my neck. "She *can't* fucking be prepared for that shit. I know women who have lived it. It fucking breaks something inside them."

"Lanea is a warrior. She is far stronger than most women." Two Case's bronzed face remained implacable.

Crank surged to his feet, fists clenched. "That fucking makes it worse." He paced for a moment, running his hands through his hair. "A while back, we busted up a sex trafficking thing. Several of the women who had been fucking sex slaves for the Saxons MC ended up coming back home with us. Some of them..." He shook his head. "They're fucked up forever."

Two Case's expression softened a little. "I know. But those women had no choice. They were taken. Lanea has a choice. She went into this knowing what would happen, and she accepted that as the cost of the justice she wants. Her strength will allow her to endure."

"I'm glad you're so fucking sure of that." Crank sighed, sounded defeated. "What the fuck ever, man. I won't interfere unless she says. But you fucking remember, she will have to deal with this shit for a very long time." He dropped back into his chair.

It pained me to see him this way. Crank wasn't the type of man to give up on anything, especially something he believed to be true. Accepting this really hurt him.

The need to comfort him rose within me, and before I could rethink the impulse, I went to him and wrapped my arms around him. "It'll be as okay as we can make it, Crank."

He glanced up at me, and slid his hand along my arm. "Yeah, well, I'm not so fucking sure I can live with that. I should have just fucking killed Sennit and called it good enough."

"But then those other men would have continued what they're doing. Killing Sennit might slow them down for a short time, but they would easily find another way. This way allows us to stop them from hurting more children, too." He had to see the big picture. Getting too bogged down in the details of Lanea's situation tormented him too much to allow him to care for the other victims.

He nodded. "Yeah, but I could have made Sennit give me their names, and fucking killed them, too. Problem fucking solved."

My heart clenched at the pain in his voice. "No, that wouldn't solve it. Eventually, you would get caught. And while morally, you would be right, the legal system would have a field day with a member of a biker gang killing random upstanding citizens, even if it were vigilante justice."

His automatic defense of the Hell Raiders kicked in. "It's not a gang. The Hell Raiders is a club. Big difference."

"Semantics, and you know it. Calling it a club doesn't change how the rest of the world sees it. You would be crucified, and the police would be all over every biker gang in the country, searching for more killers. The rest of society would be in a panic, and any time they saw someone on a motorcycle, their fear would conjure up all kinds of scenarios, which they would report as fact. It would become a witch hunt." I paused a second for that to sink in. "This way, you get to stop them, and the police get the credit."

"You could be right." The admission seemed painful for him. "But that doesn't mean I have to fucking like it."

"No, it doesn't. And you wouldn't be the man I know you are if you did like it." Relief started to bring my nerves under control. He wouldn't do anything rash, at least for now.

Tension filled his muscles and he gently, but firmly, shrugged my arms away. "You don't fucking know anything about me, Sarah." The cold tone sent a shiver down my spine.

I had to search for the anger that propelled me to take action and fight for him, but I found it. "I know more about you than you know about yourself."

His eyes blazed as he turned to face me. "No. You have some romantic idea of who you fucking think I am. That's not me."

I laughed. "Oh, I have no illusions about who and what you are, James Harrison Baer. You might think you hide behind what you show the world, but I know the *real* you." I refused to take it further there, in front of the other men. I turned to Two Case. "I'm going back to my room, unless you intend to hold a gun to my head again any time soon?"

Two Case shook his head and held one hand up. "No, ma'am."

"Good." I turned on my heel and marched out the door before the tears could escape.

When I finally closed the door to the room I shared with Crank behind me, I collapsed and let the sobs come. He still cared. I knew it. He showed it in the moments his guard was down. But whatever obstacle he had decided lay between us, he seemed determined to keep it there. How did I stand a chance against that?

Pain made me want my mom, but my instincts warned me away from calling her. She would be glad to hear from me, of course, but she wouldn't understand how I could care so much for a man who kept pushing me away. Her advice would be simple. Forget him and find a decent man to settle down with. As if that were even possible.

The thought of her words of wisdom prompted an idea,

though. What if Crank thought I had given up on him? Would he simply accept and go away? Or would he fight for what he really wanted and needed? The risk was too huge to even consider trying it, but I filed it away for the future, in case nothing else worked.

Melissa. Maybe she would have an idea. I dried my tears, blew my nose, and splashed cold water on my face. Annoyed with the damage the crying jag wrought on my makeup, I washed the rest of it off. It failed to do its job anyway. Finally, somewhat composed, I made the call.

She answered on the first ring. "Are you okay? Jackie said you were sick? What's wrong? Why didn't you call me? Did things go okay with the biker?"

The flood of questions finally ended, allowing me to reply. "I'm not sick. And it was amazing until last night." I told her, trying to hold more tears back. It felt good to share with someone, but it hurt, too.

"Oh, honey. I'm sorry. I so hoped it would be different." My best friend's quiet words of comfort helped. "Tell me his name. I'll make his life a living nightmare."

A small laugh escaped. "No, you don't have to do that. I just need to figure out how to get through to him." So typical of Melissa to want to beat up anyone who hurt me.

"You really care for this guy that much?"

"Mel, I think I love him." And there it was. The 'L' word, given life by the act of speaking it. "I don't know what to do."

"Does he feel the same for you? I mean, I know you said he talked about a future, and growing old together, but that could just be blowing smoke. Some guys will do that." From her tone, she thought that's exactly what Crank had done.

"I think he does." Did he really? Or had it all been a fairy tale designed to get him whatever he wanted from me? "I don't know."

"Well, that's the first question you have to answer. Then you'll know how to go forward." We talked longer, about Crank and the things he had said to me, and about possible ways to determine how he really felt. "Bitch, I have to go for now, have to leave for a visit. Call me tonight if you can, and you can catch me up on your progress."

The whole situation with Lanea flashed through my mind. "I'm not sure when I'll be able to call. I don't want to while he's around, just in case he overhears." The excuse sounded lame.

"Don't wait too long. I want to hear more. And Sarah?"

"Yes?"

"You take care of yourself. Don't let this guy hurt you again."

"I'll try." Too late.

We said goodbye, and I sat there on the bed, trying to compose myself. It was only early afternoon, and exhaustion already tugged hard at my mind. Despair weakened my resistance, and I lay back to close my eyes and rest a moment. Maybe a twenty-minute power nap would refresh me, and allow me to face the rest of the day.

I woke, groggy and confused, to a pitch-dark room and the sound of the door rattling as someone opened it. Fear flooded my mind, and I stayed still, frozen in helplessness. The gun Crank gave me sat in my bag on the other side of the room, useless against the intruder.

The door opened, and faint light silhouetted a male form in the frame for just a second before he closed it soundlessly.

My heart pounded in my throat as I searched my mind for some defense. Why hadn't he turned on a light? Surely a random burglar would want to know what he picked up?

But what if he wasn't there to steal anything? Could Sennit have tracked me down and sent someone to kill me? Yes. Definitely, yes. A killer might not need light.

I struggled to listen, every sound magnified. Water dripped in the bathroom. A muffled TV played in the next room. My own breathing was harsh and rapid.

And someone else breathed calmly, not at all shaken by the darkness.

CHAPTER 24

Crank:

Sarah's phone went to voice mail for the fifth time. "Fuck." I turned toward Two Case. "I have to go, man. Something's wrong with Sarah. She's not picking up." The effort to keep the panic out of my voice left my hands shaking.

"It's all good, man. She's probably in the shower or something, but you should check anyway. Nothing going on here now, anyway."

I left, relying heavily on my martial arts training to regulate my fucking heart rate. Damn thing wanted to pound straight out of my chest. I normally wasn't the sort to be spooked in any kind of situation, but going around the side of that rundown motel in the waning light broke a fine sweat over my whole body.

What the fuck would I do if something had happened to Sarah? Hell, for all I knew, she just got sick of my shit and left on her own. Or she could have gone to Sennit to try and take care of things herself, and save Lanea any more trauma. Good thing she hadn't heard what went on this afternoon. I would never shake the sound of that girl's sobs when that motherfucker raped her.

I tried to put the worst case scenario out of my head, but it refused to leave me the fuck alone. A noise across the parking lot had me pulling my gun, but it turned out to be a fucking cat scrabbling at the dumpster. A deep breath did nothing to settle my damn nerves. What if Sennit had figured shit out and sent his thugs after her?

I was a fucking idiot to leave her alone like that, defenseless. I frantically calculated the time since she left Two Case's room. Over six hours. They could have taken her anywhere in that amount of time. When I finally reached the room, it lay in pitch darkness, not even the bathroom light left on.

Nothing moved in the dark room. Fuck. Where was she? All the crazy shit kept running through my head. Had she gone home despite the risk to her safety? Or had my stupidity chased her away? The possibilities brought more sweat to my forehead, even though I tried to keep my shit together.

Then I heard it. Rapid, shallow breathing. Someone else was in the room, and scared. "Sarah?"

"Crank? Is that you?" Her shaky voice weakened my muscles with relief.

I found the light switch and the dim lamp in the corner came on. "You okay?"

She clutched the blanket up under her chin, but when she saw me, she relaxed visibly, and sat up. "Yes, I am now. You startled me."

"I got worried, and your phone kept going to voice mail." Fuck me. I was a fucking idiot. I crossed to the bed and sat by her. "I'm fucking sorry I was such a douchebag." I wrapped her into my arms, determined to never let her go again, no matter what.

"I'm sorry, I fell asleep." My shoulder muffled her words. "And yes, you were a douchebag." She pulled back enough to look up at me, searching my face. "What happened? Why did you change like that?"

How the fuck could I explain something that seemed so

logical at the time, but sounded fucking stupid now? "Would you believe I'm a fucking idiot?"

Her soft chuckle warmed me with relief. "I would, but I know you're not."

"You might not be ready to hear this." Fuck, would she judge me, and decide she didn't want me after all?

"Give me a chance, Crank." Her voice cracked a little. "I need to know what happened."

Fuck me, but I told her. All of it. The football coach she was supposed to marry, the kids she was supposed to have, and the way the MC life chewed good women up and spit them out. "Sarah, I would rather hurt you now, lose you now, than to see you hurt by my life. You deserve the best of everything, and I'm not the man who can give you that." The more I said, the more pissed she looked. I was talking myself into a fucking big, deep hole. "I'm sorry for all of it. I never intended to hurt you."

She sat there in silence for a long fucking time. "I don't even know what to say." She looked up at me, eyes full of anger. "But I think I have the right to choose my own future. The last I heard, women were no longer treated like property or livestock in this country."

Damn. I fucked up. Bad. "I'm sorry. I thought I was doing what was best for you." I had no other fucking defense.

"I know you did. But how about you consult me the next time you want to decide something that effects my life?" She sighed a little, and tightened her lips, as if she wanted to say more, but held it in. "Crank, I know this is new to you. It's new to me, too. I don't know how this happened. It's overwhelming, and I have no idea how to process it. But I do know if we don't talk, we can't make it work."

Fuck. My woman was smart as hell. I had no fucking clue what to say, so I just nodded. I'd figure it out later.

"Crank, you can't just nod. You have to say something."

Well, shit. "I...uh...okay, yeah, I'm sorry." The temperature in the room went up a few hundred degrees and sweat broke over my upper lip. "You're completely right."

My damn phone started buzzing. Pissed at the interruption, I glanced at the screen anyway. Two Case. "What?"

"Get over here." Then dead air.

"Two Case has something. Come on." While Sarah pulled her clothes on, I threw all our shit back in our bags, and double checked my weapons.

"Ready." She pulled her hair back in a ponytail. One glimpse of the way her shirt stretched over her tits, and I cussed Two Case for his bad timing.

I unhappily adjusted my half-hard dick, and grabbed our bags, keeping one hand free for a gun. Outside, the security light over the parking lot flickered randomly in the deepening darkness. The building muffled traffic sounds from the street. The whole thing felt eerie as fuck. The hair on the back of my neck stood up, and I watched carefully for signs of a threat. I'd learned long ago to trust my instincts.

"Stay close." The bags over my shoulder made it awkward, but I kept that hand on Sarah's arm. I had no intention of allowing someone to take her in a snatch and grab.

Her surprised grunt served as my only warning before a force hit the middle of my back and propelled me against the side of the building. Spinning, I used the bags as a weapon, and caught the attacker about chest high. It was enough to slow him down. Pushing Sarah behind me, I allowed my training to take over.

A slashing downward blow with the butt of the gun caught one fucker on the side of the neck, and he went down hard. A kick contacted the solar plexus of the other one, doubling him over to take a knee to the face. In a matter of seconds, the threat was cleared.

I grabbed the bags, and Sarah's arm again. "Stay fucking close, and run." I shortened my strides to accommodate hers, and practically dragged her to Two Case's room. I smacked the window as I passed. "Open up. Coming in hot."

The door swung open and I gave Sarah an unceremonious shove inside, then kicked it shut behind me.

Two Case helped Sarah to her feet as I dropped the damn bags. "What's going on? Besides you coming in here like a lunatic."

"Two thugs tried to get the drop on us coming out of our room."

"Sennit?"

"I don't know. Could have been, but if it was, he didn't send the good help." I gave a quick re-cap. "I didn't take the time to check them out."

"I'll get it. We have some extra hands right now." He placed a quick call, said a few words, and hung up. "If they're still there, the boys will get to the bottom of it."

A small sound drew my attention back to Sarah. She huddled at the end of the bed, tears rolling down her cheeks, hands shaking as she tried to still them in her lap.

With a sick feeling in the pit of my gut, I sat down beside her and pulled her close. "It's okay now. You're safe."

She nodded. "I know. I...I was just scared." Her whole fucking body trembled against me.

"Hey, Gator, you got any liquor? She could use a shot." I wrapped both arms around her and lifted her into my lap.

Gator brought over a fifth of Jack, and a plastic motel water cup, still wrapped in plastic. He got the cup opened and poured three fingers. "Here, Sarah, you drink all this. It'll help you feel better."

I helped her hold the cup, and she got the first gulp down, then gasped at the force of the alcohol hitting her throat. After a lot of coaxing, she managed to get the whole thing down. But the tremors had already subsided.

Two Case stepped back a little from the post he'd taken at the window. "All good now?"

"Yeah, what's up?"

"It's going down tomorrow. Sennit liked Lanea enough to include her in his scheduled sale tomorrow. Her and several other kids go to at least six paying customers. He gave her all kinds of warnings about what would happen if she opened her mouth about not wanting to be there." Two Case scowled. "Also got his name on tape. He got a call and answered during the conversation."

"That's good then for turning it over to the feds." I still had no intention of allowing anyone else to punish Sennit, and I figured Two Case and Gator felt the same way. They nodded in silent reply to my unasked question. Yeah, same idea. "So what's our plan?"

"We don't have an exact location yet, though Sennit mentioned something called the Wilmott. Assume that's a hotel. Gator is running it down now." Two Case went on with how everything should go down.

When he finished, I nodded, considering. "Yeah, that should cover everything." They'd made a solid plan of action, accounting for variables that may or may not come into play.

A soft tap at the door interrupted, followed by a few words in a language I didn't recognize. Two Case seemed to, though. He crossed and let a kid inside, who looked about seventeen or so.

The kid glanced around, did a double take when his gaze landed on Sarah, then turned back to Two Case. "Couple of junkies, looking for easy cash."

"You're sure?"

"Of course, motherfucker. I don't make that kind of mistake. They had a little on them, though, so they're on a payroll and following orders." The kid grinned as if he'd pulled off some big prank, then spun to face Sarah. "My name is Storm, if you ever need anything. Your man did a good job, laid those cocksuckers out cold. They both need a medicine man."

Two Case shook his head. "Get the fuck out of here, kid. If I need anything else, I'll send a smoke signal."

The kid grinned again, gave a mock salute, and left without making a sound.

"Excuse him." Two Case turned the lock on the door and glanced out the window. "He's young and...enthusiastic."

Gator gave a muffled laugh. "Yeah, that's one way to put it. Little fucker is bloodthirsty."

Two Case agreed and they joked back and forth for a moment, until Sarah gathered her composure enough to speak. "You, all of you, sound like this..." She gestured around with her hands. "All of this, is just business as usual. I don't even know what to think about that."

"Sarah, darlin', it kind of is business as usual." I tried to think how to put it. "The difference is, we're coming down on the right side this time. We're one-percenters. We live outside the law, and we break it all the fucking time. Usually, we're breaking the law, or figuring out how to skirt it."

She shrugged a little. "I thought that sort of thing was only on TV."

And there it was. She couldn't accept my life, even though before she thought she could. I should have known better than get my hopes up. It was okay, though. I couldn't expect her to just turn against everything she'd ever fucking known.

"For most people, it is. For me, and others like me, it's fucking everyday life. I told you before, Sarah, I'm not a good man."

She stared up at me for a moment. "I don't care what kind of life you lead. I know you're a good man when it counts."

CHAPTER 25

Sarah:

My head spun with everything that happened in the last couple of hours. I was more than ready when Crank led me back to our room. As we walked, the memory of that man's hands on me earlier made me jump at every shadow or little noise. Crank seemed to sense my fear, and pulled me closer.

I tried to slow my heart rate by remembering the speed and effectiveness of Crank's actions against the attackers. They hadn't had a chance with him. He warned me before that he was a dangerous man. He hadn't lied. Maybe that should frighten me, but it had the opposite effect. I felt entirely safe with Crank. He wouldn't allow anything or anyone to harm me. And he had the skills to back it up. By the time we reached our room, I was okay.

He closed the door behind us, and put our bags back on the dresser. "Guess we didn't need all this shit after all. Figured we should take it though, just in case."

I watched him pull his boots off, suddenly wary. Had the Crank I loved really returned? Or that cold and distant stranger? Acknowledging the emotion surprised me a little. It felt new and unfamiliar, but strong and ready to flourish. All it needed was him.

His leather vest followed his boots, and then his T-shirt came off to reveal the ridges and planes of his chest and abs. Even after I knew what he tasted like, what his skin felt like, and traced the swirling lines of his tattoos, the view still left me unable to do anything more than watch him. Another realization came to me with startling clarity. He was a drug, and I was the junkie.

I stood, my mouth dry and my pulse fluttering wildly, and started peeling my own clothes off. He loosened his jeans and stared at me like a starving beast, ready to devour me. And I wanted to be consumed, more than I wanted to keep breathing. Naked, I faced him, already breathing hard, waiting. My breasts felt full and heavy, needing his touch, while the ache at my center expanded.

He stared at me, chest rising and falling steadily, and his gaze flicked over my body in an intimate touch that felt physical. "Are you sure you're ready for this, Sarah?" His voice sounded uncharacteristically rough and husky. "I won't fucking back off again. If you're mine tonight, you're mine forever. I'll do everything possible to shield you from the bad shit in my life, but it will always be there."

How strange that I didn't need even a moment to consider. "I'm sure." The old me, even at her most rebellious, would never have considered such a thing. "I don't care what else is in your life, as long as I'm there, too."

Crank crossed the room in a rush and gathered me roughly into his arms. "Thank fuck."

I couldn't get close enough to him. My body yearned for his touch, and I made some pitiful pleading noise deep in my throat.

His mouth came down on mine with almost bruising force, and I met him more than halfway. A sharp nip at my upper lip sent even more heat to pool in my lower regions. He took advantage of my small gasp to thrust his tongue between my lips. That velvety stroke against the sensitive skin he found made me squirm against him. I never wanted that kiss to end, but I needed so much more.

He slid his hands between us, separating us a little, even as I struggled to get closer. And then he shoved his jeans down, allowing me to press against the full length of his body. A low hiss escaped him as his erection came into contact with my body, bringing me a sense of satisfaction.

Rough, calloused hands skimmed over my body, then settled just under my butt long enough for him to lift me a bit. My turn to hiss came as his erection slipped between my thighs, and he moved so it just barely caressed my outer parts. My entire lower area pulsed, incredibly aroused by the light touch.

"Fuck, baby, so hot!" His hot breath against my neck made me whimper with need. He raised me in his arms, and took a few quick steps, then lowered me to the bed. "And for fucking once, I'm taking my time with you. By the time I'd done, you'll know exactly who you belong to." The words made me shiver with anticipation.

***

Crank:

Fuck. She fucking destroyed me with the little noises she made. The only consolation was she seemed as deeply affected by me as I was by her. With one knee on the bed beside her, I leaned down to taste her mouth again, before I moved on to other delicacies. She gave a little moan and wrapped her arms around my neck.

"Mmm, no baby. Going on my schedule this time." I untangled her arms and drew away a little, just enough to lick down her neck and settle on one nipple. She arched as I applied a little pressure with my teeth and flicked my tongue over her sensitive flesh.

I continued, fucking determined to find everything she didn't know she loved. A scrape of my teeth on the underside of her tit brought a frustrated groan as she tried to guide me back to her nipple.

In sheer self-defense, so I didn't give in and let her have what she wanted and bring this to an end way too fucking soon, I pulled back, out of reach. "Keep that up, baby, and I'll have to punish you."

She looked up at me, maybe a little worried, but her eyes stayed dark with desire, and her lips parted. "Punish?"

Fuck, I hoped she pushed it. "Yeah. You know that thing that happens when you do shit you're not supposed to."

"Oh." She stared at me a little longer. "Okay."

I switched to the other nipple, and teased the first with my fingers, and just like that, she pulled at my hair, trying to guide me again. I let her nipple pop out of my mouth. "Ah, ah, I warned you."

A touch of fear widened her eyes. "I'm sorry."

"Too late for sorry." I backed off the bed and drew her to the edge. "Now you get the fucking consequences." Leaning over her, I stroked my cock along her tit, concentrating on the nipple. Fuck! Why did I feel like the one being tortured?

She moaned again, small hands reaching for my hard-on, wanting more. For just an instant, I gave in, and let her, then pulled back again. Lifting her gently, I turned her, and flipped her to her belly, then raised her to her hands and knees.

That perfect ass offered way too fucking much temptation. I brought my palm down on it with a light smack. Sarah gasped in shock, but now that she was prepared, I gave it another smack, a little harder, then stopped to rub away the sting.

"You spanked me!" Her indignation almost made me laugh.

My fingers dipped to her wet slit, silencing her objections with another gasp. "Yeah, and you fucking liked it." One finger slipped inside her, and the reflexive clench of her muscles nearly undid me. The sight of my handprint standing out in pink relief against her pale skin did it. I lined up and slid the head of my dick along her slit, then paused at her entrance for only a second. So much for waiting.

Sarah met me more than half way, thrusting back onto my hard-on with a sound that curled my toes. I caught one arm around her waist and drew her fully onto her knees as I pushed deep, groaning at the impossible tightness of the angle. Wrapping her hair around my other hand, I angled her head back and to the side so I could taste her mouth again.

She whimpered when I increased the pressure on her hair, and her internal muscles squeezed hard. I let my hand at her waist slip down to circle her clit with one finger, bringing on another spasm.

"Fuck, baby, how you keep doing this to me?" I lowered her back to her hands and knees, but kept my grip on her hair, and my finger strumming that little bundle of nerves. Her only reply was a wordless cry, and she thrust back onto me, hard.

More than ready, I gave myself over to her. Our skin slapped together, punctuated by my harsh breathing and her sounds of abandon, pushing me to drive harder. Even the fucking smell of sex with Sarah was different, addictive, and enough to keep me on edge forever.

My head buzzed with desperate need for release, and she gave a sudden cry, sharper than before, and her body seized up, inner muscles rippling on my cock as she rode the crest of her orgasm. And that's all it took. Heat exploded at the base of my spine and my muscles went rigid, keeping me in place as I poured into her. Finally, I slumped forward over her, and we both concentrated on just getting enough air into our lungs.

She moved a little, and I allowed her to turn over, then dropped to the soft cradle her body offered. "Crank?"

"Mmm?" Any other words refused to form.

"I love you."

Shit! I raised my head, looking down at her. She looked thoroughly fucking satisfied, happy, but a little nervous. She was hardly the first chick to say that word to me, but she was the first I took seriously. And the first I felt the same thing back for.

She shook her head. "I'm sorry. I shouldn't have said that." She bit her lip and tears filled her eyes.

Leave it to me to fucking wait too long. "Fuck, Sarah, no don't cry. Please." I rolled to the side and gathered her close. "You startled me a little. I've never had someone say that to me and actually mean it."

She pushed back from me. "No, it's okay. You don't have to explain, or anything. I got carried away."

Now how the fuck was I supposed to fix this shit? "Sarah—"

"No, really, Crank." She turned away, but not before a fucking tear spilled over. "I'm tired. Goodnight."

Fuck. Fuck. Fuck. This amazing proud woman actually loved me, and all I could do was fucking hurt her. A goddamn lump the size of a Harley engine filled my throat. I fell back against my pillow in defeat, and for the first time since I killed Old Man Hardymon on that crooked mountain road, fucking tears of pain leaked from my eyes.

CHAPTER 26

Sarah:

Tears soaked my pillow, and I didn't even have the will to wipe them from my eyes. He'd broken me. In just seconds. Maybe he was right. He was a bad man, and I would do well to keep my distance. Except even while my heart shattered, every fiber of my being craved him.

And he lay there beside me, his body still, his breathing even and deep as he slept. Not even a hint of regret, beyond that moment after I first said it. No doubt that came from embarrassment more than any kind of feeling for me.

First thing tomorrow, I would talk to Gator and Two Case. There was really no need for me to be here any longer. I could creep away and lick my wounds in private, while they took care of Sennit however they chose.

One side of me, the little girl with the boo-boos, wanted her mommy to kiss it all better, the real me knew I could never share this with my mom. She wouldn't let it go, and every time she thought I might be on the brink of taking a risk, she would pull it out to remind me of the consequences.

No matter how badly I hurt now, I found no anger in my heart for Crank. He was just living his life the only way he knew how. In fact, a sort of gratitude filled me. In the brief time I knew him, he had shown me what it was like to be treasured. No regrets.

For the first time in my life, I understood how some

women tolerated absolutely anything from a man, just to keep him. An empty, bleak future stretched before me, without Crank. If he offered the opportunity to stay with him right now, what sacrifices was I prepared to make? I had already given up any measure of self-respect. And suddenly, the unfathomable prospect of numbing my heart and mind with drugs seemed like a reasonable thing. Was this how people fell into that life?

God, I couldn't believe how stupid I was, to just blurt it out like that. No warning. No hints. And he had only just come back to me from whatever dark place he went while he thought he was no good for me. For the rest of my life, the memory of that impulse would haunt me. Along with the what-ifs. What if I waited? What if I let him say it first? What if I just took what he gave, and loved him silently?

I should hate the day I met him, but I couldn't. Something changed in me then. Later, even after he hurt me so badly by ignoring my messages, when trouble came, my instincts still demanded I call him. Before Crank, if I saw something wrong or illegal, I never hesitated to contact law enforcement. What was it about him that changed me so deeply? It was a stupid question. I knew the answer already. My heart belonged to him from the moment he began to flirt with me so outrageously. I just didn't realize it at the time.

A long time later, with my heart aching, I slipped out of the bed and went to hide in the bathroom. The shower concealed the sounds of the sobs that refused to hold off any longer. But even that small space no longer held refuge. The many times Crank and I made love under the spray of water were indelibly printed on my mind. The beat of water on my skin catapulted me back in time to relive those experiences.

Eventually, unable to wallow in self-pity any longer, I shut the water off, and took my time getting dressed for whatever lay ahead. Oddly, this time, my grief left little evidence on my face. It felt wrong for my heart to lie in tatters, while I showed no outward sign. But if that's what it took to give me the strength to get through what lay ahead, I would take it.

When no further excuse to hide in the bathroom remained, I opened the door, hoping to stay silent and not disturb Crank. Maybe I could even slip from the room before he woke.

Stepping out into the still dark room, I came up hard against a wall of muscle, and large hands rescued me from falling. A startled half-scream left my lips.

"Sarah. It's me. Calm down." Crank's reassuring rumble threatened to break down the meager defenses I'd built.

I pulled away. "Sorry. All yours now." I moved to step around him, but he caught me to him.

"Sarah, I'm sorry."

"Don't worry about it. My fault." This time when I tried to go around him, to my great relief, he allowed it.

"Make no mistake, Sarah, we're going to talk about this. But right now, I have to piss, really bad. So you have a minute." He disappeared into the bathroom, closing the door behind him.

One glance out the window at the parking lot, still in heavy shadows, killed my determination to leave the room. Besides, my heart was already destroyed. He couldn't do much more damage, so I might as well let him assuage his guilty conscience. At least he could get on with his life without feeling too badly.

I stood there a moment in the dark, unsure where to sit. The bed seemed far too suggestive, so I settled into one of the straight chairs by the little table.

He came out of the bathroom, flipped on a bedside lamp, and settled onto the bed, as naked as when he went to sleep last night. "Over here, Sarah." He patted the bed at his side. "What I have to say isn't easy, and I don't want to have to try to be heard."

How could I be that close to his nakedness and not touch? Self-preservation kicked in. I bolted, fumbling with the lock, but reaching freedom. He couldn't come after me naked, someone might see him. I paused to look back.

He stood shameless in the doorway. "Sarah, I'm not fucking playing. Don't make me come get you." One raised eyebrow testified to his seriousness.

I ran. Surely Two Case or Gator would help me.

The only warning came as a soft sound behind me before strong arms wrapped around my waist. Crank's familiar scent overwhelmed my senses. "Goddamn, Sarah, you're going to fucking listen if it kills me." He swung me over his shoulder and started walking. Inside the room, he put me down, but kept himself between me and the door. "Sit on the fucking bed."

I shrugged. "Fine." I moved to the bed, and took a seat on the edge, as far from his side as possible. "What is it?"

He gave a dark chuckle as he sat down. "Sarah, I'm not going to molest you, or some shit like that. Relax."

Stifling a sigh, I complied, leaning back against the headboard. "Better?"

"Not much, but it'll fucking do." He moved his pillow, and turned, putting his feet at the top of the headboard, then lay back, knees bent, so he could look straight up into my face. "Like I said, I need to say something, and it isn't easy. I'd rather do it face to face, but this works, too."

Intrigued despite my need to maintain some distance, I

shrugged. "Okay?"

He took a deep breath. "I told you a little about how I grew up. I left out the part about the girls." Another deep breath. "I was pretty big for my age, and tall. The first time, I was twelve, I think. I'd always fucking known what my old man was, but I wasn't prepared for older kids wanting shine or weed, and being willing to do anything to get it for cheap."

A nagging sense of horror built in my stomach, but I stayed silent.

"An older girl on the bus, maybe sixteen, said she had something really cool to show me, but only if I got her a quart of shine. Curious about what an older girl might want to show me, I did it. I didn't know shit about sex, beyond the very basics, but I fucking enjoyed that first head job. The next day, I heard her joking with her friends about blowing the shiner's kid for a free quart. That was the beginning." He paused for another deep breath.

Fear for that little boy, and dread for what he faced, filled me, but still, I kept quiet, and waited.

"They offered anything and everything. Sex. Other drugs. Even love. I learned real fast that love was a fucking myth. It was something to use to get what you wanted. Later, I wasn't above using it myself, though I couldn't bring myself to actually say it. After my old man died, I had a rep. By then, I could get anything a chick wanted, for a price. Somewhere along the way, probably when I was going to college, I fucking realized what I'd been. But after that wreck, I didn't give a flying fuck any more. Bitches came and went, willing to do or say anything for a chance to be a Hell Raider's ol' lady." He closed his eyes for a moment, and something that could have been a tear squeezed from between his lids.

At that point, I loved him more than before, if that were

even possible. But he didn't seem finished, so I waited, and fought the urge to comfort him.

"I went on about my life, fucking any bitch that came along hot enough to suit me, but I knew, without a fucking doubt, whenever one of my brothers fell for some chick, they were getting taken. Love couldn't exist, otherwise, no one would throw it around so fucking carelessly. But then, I met you." Deep breath again. "Suddenly, I knew. I fell in love with you the moment you glared at me like you wanted to scratch my eyes out. I just never expected to get it back."

My own tears slid unchecked down my cheeks.

He moved for the first time, taking my hand. "Sarah, I fucked up, in more ways than one. I know that. It might kill me, but I understand if you can't forgive me for hurting you. But don't you ever doubt that I fucking love you."

Stunned, I let his words soak in. "Crank, I...I had no idea."

"Nobody did. I trust my brothers with my life, but not with that shit. You are the only person on this fucking earth who can truly hurt me. And I don't regret giving you that."

I struggled for words. "Crank, I could never deliberately hurt you. I was prepared to walk out of your life to spare you the discomfort of facing me this morning, because I actually do love you."

A feral sounding growl escaped him as he dragged me down into his arms, to kiss me like the world was drawing to the end and we would never have another moment.

CHAPTER 27

Crank:

A long while after my confession, I lay there with a sleeping Sarah nestled in my arms, just thinking. Why did it take the prospect of truly losing her forever for me to talk to her? I could have saved us both a lot of heartache by just saying it. For the life of me, though, I thought she knew I loved her. Sure I hadn't said the words, but I did say we were forever, and she was mine. Apparently, that didn't mean the same fucking thing.

My phone buzzed and I ignored the fucker. Lying there with a warm and sated Sarah cuddled up close was my only fucking goal in life. The damn thing finally fell silent, and I started to doze off, until a thunderous pounding started at the door.

"Crank, open up." Two Case's voice echoed through the room. Fuck, half the town probably heard him.

Sarah slept on, so I slid from the bed, trying not to wake her. It took a minute, but I found my jeans and opened the door. I signaled Two Case for quiet and stepped aside to let him in.

After a quick glance at the bed, he nodded. "Glad you got that sorted out. But I've been trying to call you for over an hour."

"Sorry, man. Must have dozed off."

"Sennit is picking Lanea and a couple of the other girls

up at noon. Figured you might need a little wakeup call after your morning jog."

I chuckled. "Should have known you had someone watching." I glanced back at Sarah. "Have to admit, this is getting wrapped up faster than I expected." More like I hoped it might take a little longer. Yeah, that wasn't good for Lanea, but it would give me more time with Sarah without having to explain other things about my life.

"Yeah, I didn't either. I have Runner and Storm, along with a couple of others, watching and ready to follow. Just be ready to roll at eleven-thirty, and we'll be right behind them when they get there." He glanced toward the bed again. "Even though I would rather not have a civilian involved in this shit storm, we might need her to help with some of the kids."

I nodded. "Yeah, fucking truth there. We'll be over at the other room before eleven-thirty." A fist-bump later, I closed the door behind him and locked it, then turned back to the bed. We had just over an hour to get ready, and I needed to get Sarah something to eat. Couldn't have her fucking fainting from hunger in the middle of cleaning this shit up.

I sat on the edge of the bed beside her and pulled a little of the sheet down to expose the curve of her back. That satin skin could hold my full attention for fucking ever. Fascinated by the texture, I ran a fingertip down her spine. It must have tickled, because she squirmed just a little, then went still again, sleeping soundly.

Would she get inked for me? Just the thought of my fucking name on her skin gave me a raging hard-on. Ol' Lester did some beautiful work on the ol' ladies, and whichever chicks wanted ink. He had a way of working script in with the skulls and flames of the Hell Raiders, and adding detailed roses to give it a feminine touch, that fucking surpassed any other inkslinger in the region.

If she agreed to a tattoo, where would he choose to put my name on Sarah? Most of the ol' ladies had the ink on their arms, clearly visible, but a couple had larger, more detailed pieces on their backs as well. I wanted everyone to see that Sarah belonged to me, so a forearm would be best. But my fucking name trailing along the length of her spine? The idea made me instantly need to be balls deep inside her. Too bad we had a fucking schedule to keep. One more thing to punish Sennit for.

With no more time to waste, I stroked more firmly along her back. "Time to rise and shine, baby."

She stirred a little and smiled. "Mmm. Keep doing that."

My dick surged in my jeans, but instead of following orders, I flipped the sheet back further and smacked her lightly on the ass. "No time. We have to be ready to roll in an hour, and I thought you might want to shower first."

Startled, she turned over to pout at me. "Roll? It's time already?"

"We're going to take Sennit's ass out today."

My words acted like a NOX injection to a street racer. She sat bolt upright. "Why didn't you say so? I can be ready in ten minutes."

"Nah, you don't have to rush that much. It's a little after ten now, and we don't need to meet Two Case and Gator until eleven-thirty. You have time for a good hot shower, and I'll go get us something to eat while you do that." I had to fucking leave the room when she went into that shower, or I would be in there fucking her up against the wall, and any other way I could get her. Memory of water cascading down her back while I pounded into her had my dick trying mightily to break out of prison. I leaned in for a quick kiss. "I'll see you in a few minutes."

She let the sheet drop completely and started for the bathroom, naked and tempting, while I tried to distract myself with pulling on clean socks. "Crank?" She paused at the door, looking back over her shoulder.

"Yeah, baby?" Fuck, if she asked me to wash her back, our schedule would be shot all to hell.

"I love you." She said it, just like that, as if it were the most normal fucking thing in the world.

Those three words sent my pulse hammering into my dick. "I love you too, Sarah. Don't you ever fucking doubt that." Pushed beyond my limits for discomfort, I reached into my jeans to adjust myself. "And just so you know, any time you want me to fuck you, that's all you have to say."

She disappeared into the bathroom with a giggle, closing the door behind her.

I took a deep, steadying breath as the shower came on. Fuck, that woman would be the death of me, and I would go out with a hard-on. By the time I pulled on a clean t-shirt and ran my fingers over my hair to put it in something like order, I had myself under slightly better control. I shrugged into my cut, checked my weapons, and stepped into my boots quickly, in a hurry to get the fuck back to my woman.

Outside, I needed my shades to cut the glare of the morning sun before I headed down the street to the little diner. Hopefully, they had coffee and breakfast. More people moved around in the area than I had seen before, mostly older folks, some dragging yappy little fucking dogs around on leashes. One such ankle-biter snarled and growled at me like a fucking pit guarding a stash. I growled back and the little bastard yelped and dodged behind the old gal leading him.

The old woman laughed. "There, Tiger, I told you that

shit would get you bitten." She grinned at me. "Thanks for not kicking him. He thinks he's all badass."

I chuckled. "Gotta admire his courage anyway. He was just warning me away."

She stooped to lift the little fur ball into her arms. "Most people don't realize that, though. You must be new around here."

My turn to laugh. I liked the old gal. "I am, but I'm only here for a little while. But right now, I'm searching for coffee and breakfast. There a good place around here?"

She pointed back the way she came. "Right down there. Miss Barb's pancakes are the best in the state. Me and Tiger used to get them once a week, but we can't afford it anymore."

Fuck me. A nice old lady like that shouldn't have to worry about affording some fucking pancakes for her and her dog once a fucking week. "Well, today you can. It's on me, for all your help."

Her face lit up like New Years. "Oh, son, you don't have to do that."

"I know, but I got a couple extra bucks, and can't think of a better way to spend them. Maybe then ol' Tiger won't try to take my leg off." Shit, I knew better than to get noticed, especially in this neighborhood. But that didn't stop me from offering my arm and escorting the old lady back down the street like some kind of fucking gentleman.

She giggled and prattled on about her friends, and Tiger's bravery while the little dog glared at me from his perch in the crook of her arm. In the diner, I told the old lady to order whatever she and Tiger wanted, winking at the surprised girl at the counter.

I ordered for Sarah and me. "Throw in a couple of extra sausage links for Tiger. Little shit is hungry." After I paid, I sat at one of the little tables with the old lady and Tiger. To my surprise, no one objected to the dog's presence inside the diner.

"My name is Glory, by the way, at least, that's what they call me to my face."

I couldn't hold back another chuckle. "We're in the same boat then. They call me Crank, but most call me other shit behind my back."

She offered a fragile hand across the table. "Well, Crank, I'm pleased to meet you. We don't get many MC boys around here, now that my Jake Brake is gone. After he died, his boys all moved on."

I raised an eyebrow in surprise. "You were an ol' lady?"

A proud nod served as the only necessary reply. "Can I ask you a favor? I know you're not obligated but—"

"What do you need, Glory? I'll see to it, if I possibly can."

She glanced around at the other patrons, then leaned forward and lowered her voice. "There's this man, lives right down there." She nodded in the general direction of the hotel. "Him and his woman take in foster kids, and they put up a good front, but somethin' ain't right. He's hurting them kids."

"How do you know?" No fucking doubt, she was talking about Lanea's 'foster father'.

She glanced around again. "I've seen a couple of the girls come running out of there, crying. The one I got a good look at, her mouth was all swollen, and she had semen on her face. Ain't no way she blew that bastard willingly."

I attempted to swallow back my rage. "What would you like to see happen to him, Glory?"

Her grin seemed surprisingly bloodthirsty for a sweet little old lady. "Well, I'd like to see him took care of like my Jake Brake would have done. He'd have cut out his balls and give 'em to the dogs. But I'll settle for a beat-down and a warning, if you could do it."

I winked at her. "Consider it done, Glory. Before I leave town, the fucker won't want to look at another kid, ever. And you give ol' Jake Brake my regards."

Her laugh turned a few heads. "I will surely do that, son. And thank you."

The counter girl called out our order number, putting an end to the conversation. Maybe Two Case had someone who could look out for the old gal.

CHAPTER 28

Crank:

Once Sarah and I finished eating, the clocked ticked over to eleven twenty. Time to get over to Two Case's room. I dropped our shit in the SUV, because I had no intention of returning to the hotel after we finished. The climate might be just a little too fucking hot in that area for me when the officials learned about it all.

Two Case and Gator had torn down their whole listening-post setup, and Gator currently had earphones plugged into his cell, so maybe he'd transferred everything over to monitor that way. The pair were armed to the teeth, not bothering to conceal the weapons they carried.

"We ready?"

Two Case nodded. "Runner and Storm are already on Sennit's tail. He's picked up a couple of other kids. Runner says he used to do that, take kids from several homes on a 'field trip' to the library or zoo, or whatever, but really, they were taken to some hotel to get whored out."

"Shit. I was hoping we wouldn't have many kids to deal with during the takedown."

"Yeah, me too." Gator shoved a wicked looking fixed blade knife into a scabbard that rested across his chest. "Scared kids will make shit harder to carry out."

The cover story we concocted to allow Sarah to bring the kids in would still work. "Yeah, it will, but Sarah will be able to handle them."

A heavy pack resting on his shoulder, Two Case grunted. "We can hope. Let's get out of here." He led the way and Sarah and I went to the SUV, while Gator closed up the room. Moments later, we pulled out behind the big pickup truck with Gator at the wheel.

Light traffic leading up to the lunch hour made it easy to stay together, but it concerned me. Heavier traffic made it harder to spot a tail. Hopefully Two Case's boys knew how to switch shit up and stay out of sight.

After a few blocks, Two Case signaled and turned in at a convenience store with an attached fast-food restaurant and parked at the edge of the lot facing the street. Exactly as planned, we would wait here for word from Runner and Storm.

In the meantime, I took advantage of the time with Sarah, and caught one of her restless hands in my own. "Nervous?"

She looked at me for a long moment. "In a way, but probably not what you're thinking."

Damn, she sounded scared as hell. "Tell me."

She ducked her head a little, hiding her face from me. "What's next?" The whispered words, nearly inaudible, betrayed her worry over something big.

I searched my mind. She knew the plan, so that couldn't have her so upset. "What do you mean?"

A shaky sigh left her lips. "What's next, Crank? We get Sennit today, and that will all be finished in a day or two, at most. Then what do we do? You go back to Kentucky, and I go back home to work?"

Well, fuck. The same fucking question had plagued me since I realized I couldn't live without her. "I don't know. I fucking have to go back. I'd like to say you're going with me."

My turn to be so nervous my hands shook. "Would you leave everything for me, Sarah? Or is that asking too fucking much?"

She looked up, finally, and met my gaze. "Do you want me to?" The apprehension in her expression stunned me. How could she fucking question that?

A deep breath helped calm me a little. "Yeah, I fucking do. More than anything. I want you with me, every goddamn minute of every day. I want a home with you, a future, fucking forever." Another deep breath for courage. "Sarah Channing, will you leave all you know, and come back to Kentucky with me?"

She waited so long to reply, I started to fucking hyperventilate. What if she refused? But finally, the answer came. "Yes. I'll come back to Kentucky with you, and we will build a life together there."

The fucking console dug one of my guns painfully into my hip as I leaned to kiss her. Her mouth tasted sweeter than ever, her lips clinging to mine. I needed more, but as I thrust my tongue between those soft lips, my fucking phone started buzzing.

Eyes closed to gather my resolve, I ended the kiss and drew back. Fucking phone continued to buzz, until I fished it out of my pocket. "Yeah."

Two Case's mocking laugh greeted me. "Get your dick back in your pants. Time to roll."

"Right." I ended the call and started the SUV. "Looks like we're getting closer." Gator's big pickup pulled away, and I followed. The truck slipped into the slightly heavier traffic, and I let a few cars separate us before I pulled out.

Beside me, Sarah clutched her hands together so hard her knuckles went white. "Do you think it's all going to work? The way we planned it?" Anxiety furrowed her forehead as she looked at me.

I didn't tell her that the real plan looked little like the one she was aware of. She didn't need to know all the fucking details about what happened to Sennit and the others after we took them down. "Maybe not exactly, but it'll work. We'll get Sennit and the pedophiles he supplies. That's the only fucking thing that matters."

"You're right. I have to quit worrying about it." She exhaled slowly, and visibly forced herself to relax back into the seat.

I kept a few cars between Gator's truck and us, just in case someone paid attention. "All you have to worry about is dealing with the kids once we get started." If I were fucking honest, I was just glad I didn't have to handle the kids.

Gator and Two Case led us about twenty minutes away, then turned onto a series of back streets that took us into an increasingly rundown area. Finally, I spotted it. A motel that looked like a stiff wind would fucking blow it down, but with several cars in the parking lot. No fucking way a dive like that had a full house for any legit reason.

We rolled right on by, and around the corner. On the next block, Gator drove straight into the open door of what looked like an abandoned warehouse. I followed, resisting the urge to pull my gun when the rolling door slid closed behind the SUV. Every fucking alarm bell in my body rang full out, warning of a set up. My instincts demanded an escape route, and that had been cut off when that door closed.

Gator stopped his truck next to a line of other vehicles, and climbed out to motion me into the space next to him. Wary as fuck, I parked and shut the car off.

Gator came over as I climbed out. "Sorry about the sketchy situation. Storm and Runner found this place on a quick recon of the area. Figured it would make a good place for us to get shit together out of sight."

Sarah and I joined a dozen men standing around the hood of a beat up Pontiac, as Runner drew a rough map in the dust covering the car. "So, quick count, we have eight rooms, a kid per room, and at least one creep per room. I don't expect they'll be armed, but you never know. We need to hit all the rooms at the same time, to keep any of them from running." He went over a few more details. "Okay, we have to move. Kids been in there ten minutes already."

And just like that, we were ready. I made sure Sarah had a gun ready, kept her right behind me, and fell in with the deadly silent group of men heading toward that ramshackle motel. My fucking respect for Fergus and his operation grew by leaps and bounds. These motherfuckers had a goal in sight, and nothing would stop them from reaching it. With nothing more than hand signals, we all moved into place, ready to strike.

I steeled myself, prepared to see just about any damn kind of depravity, and hoped I could keep it the fuck out of my head. On Runner's signal, eight flimsy-ass motel room doors crashed inward under heavy boots, and startled cries rang out. Gun in hand, I shoved through the door I'd kicked open, ready to blow a fucking pedophile or two away.

A skinny middle-aged man glanced my direction. "Well, it's about time. I told Sennit I wanted a willing child, not one too scared to enjoy this." He looked at me again, and seemed to absorb that this wasn't what he thought, and his hands went up. "Is this part of the package?"

I centered the barrel of my .45 on his forehead. "What the fuck are you talking about?"

He blinked. "I called Sennit and told him there was a problem. The child won't cooperate. Is that why you're here?"

"I'm here to fucking end you, you sick fuck." My finger tightened on the trigger, taking up the small amount of slack.

The man went pale and raised his hands even higher.

Sarah edged around me and approached a kid huddled up against the side of the bed. "Hey, sweetheart, you're safe now. What's your name?" She dropped to her knees in front of the kid.

Startling green eyes in a deathly pale face flashed fear as the kid looked up. He took everything in, then took a shaky breath. "Jimmy." Something vaguely familiar nagged at my memory.

"Okay, Jimmy, we're here to help you. I want you to come with me." She rose to her feet and held out a hand.

The kid made a lunge for her and wrapped his arms around her waist, burying his face in her arm. Gently, with lots of hushed words, she led him out of the room. As soon as they were safe, I turned my focus back to the fuck-wad sitting there in front of me.

"How about you tell me what the fuck this is all about, and I consider letting you draw another breath?"

As if he suddenly understood the seriousness of the situation, the man frowned. "What did you want to know?"

"Let's start with how a child rapist like yourself finds someone like Sennit." The fucking details were the last thing I wanted, but we needed them in order to allow Two Case and the others to wipe up any mess that survived this.

He gave an awkward shrug and leaned forward. "For the record, I am not a rapist. The children I love are with me willingly. As for the rest, word gets around. People with mutual interests tend to share sources."

I laughed. "For the record, you put your dick in a minor, you're a rapist. Stand up." I jerked him roughly to his feet, and wrapped my hand around the side of his neck. "Walk. There's some boys outside looking forward to talking to you, motherfucker." With the nose of my .45 jammed hard against the base of his skull, I shoved him for the door.

Out in the parking lot, the party was wrapping up as one of Two Case's men led his prisoner to where all the pedophiles were being searched, then forced to their knees and elbows. To the left, a bunch of kids clustered around Sarah while a couple of the men watched over them, guns drawn and ready for trouble. I turned my prisoner over, and made my way in that direction, needing to reassure myself that Sarah was actually okay.

"I remember you. On the plane." The kid from the room stared up at me.

Shit. That's why he seemed familiar. It was the kid who pestered me on the plane. "Huh. I remember you too. Thought you were going to some camp, or some shit like that."

He nodded, serious as a heart attack. "Yeah. I got there, and the Sheriff was there already, shipping kids out. One of the counsellors beat a kid up, and they closed it down. When it was my turn, my mom wouldn't take me back. So they put me in foster care."

I'd be lying if I said my heart didn't break for that damn kid.

CHAPTER 29

Sarah:

The afternoon went by in a rush of getting children picked up so they could be moved to different homes. I also gave a list of the foster homes involved in this situation to Sennit's supervisor. I had to trust in the system somewhere. Hopefully, she would follow through and investigate the homes thoroughly.

Crank and the others took the prisoners to turn them in. I expected a swarm of police to descend on us, but they never arrived. Crank said it would just be simpler to take them in themselves, since they would have to give statements and turn over evidence. It made sense, even though I was pretty sure a few of the pedophiles would arrive at the police station with a few extra bruises.

The boy Crank rescued, the one who knew him, stayed close to me through it all, but said nothing. Finally, he was the only one left to take care of.

"Okay, Jimmy, let's get you settled. Which home were you in?"

"Where's that man?"

I gave him my most reassuring smile. "Don't worry, sweetie, they took the bad man to jail."

"Not him. The one that knocked the door down." The steady gaze from such a young boy unnerved me a little.

"You mean Crank?" Surprise made my voice rise a little.

He nodded. "Yeah. Him. I'll wait for him." He marched over and sat down on the crumbling curb by the motel.

It took me a moment to recover from the small act of defiance. When I did, I went over and took a seat beside him, resisting the urge to groan when bits of the concrete dug into my butt bones. "You sure know how to pick a comfortable place to sit." I waited for him to at least smile at my joke, but he didn't even acknowledge it. "Why do you want to wait for Crank?"

He propped his elbows on his knees with a little shake of his head. "He gets it. An' he'll make sure you can't send me back to that place."

His tone raised the hair on my arms. "What place, Jimmy?"

A little shrug. "The place they put me. Ain't goin' back to that shit-hole."

I raised an eyebrow at his openly belligerent attitude. "Really. And what shit-hole would that be?"

Finally, he turned to look directly at me again, then rolled his eyes. "If I tell you, you'll just send me back. They done told me that much. No way out."

It dawned on me then. "Oh, no, Jimmy, you're not going back to the same place. We'll find you another home."

He nodded. "And I'll screw up and get sent to another one. Before you know it, I'm right back there."

I refused to admit he had a point. "What happened there?"

One thin shoulder raised, and he grimaced. "The man's mean. But the woman is worse. She give me the belt yesterday for coughing at the table when I got choked."

Nausea sucked at my stomach. "The belt?"

He nodded, then turned and wriggled until he managed

to get his shirt part of the way up. The angry welts striping his thin back made my ears buzz with anger.

"Who the fuck did that to you?" Crank's angry growl came from behind me.

Jimmy repeated his story, and I told Crank how he feared getting sent back there.

"What do we do to make sure that doesn't happen?"

"The home will have to be investigated, just like the others. If the allegations are substantiated, the children will be removed, and the people no longer allowed to be foster parents." I gave him the Cliff Notes' version.

Crank glowered. "Not good enough." He turned to Jimmy. "You hungry, kid? I'm starved."

Jimmy nodded, eyes bigger than ever.

"Good. Let's go get a burger or something, and figure this shit out. You ain't going back there." And just like that, he wrapped one arm around my waist, rested the other hand atop the boy's head, and led us both toward the SUV.

"What are you doing, Crank? We can't just—"

"Kid's hungry. I'm going to feed him." To him, the matter seemed closed.

We rode in silence for half an hour, while I searched my mind for some way out of what looked like a highly illegal situation. Finally, we reached the little diner near the motel where we had stayed. Inside, we ordered at the counter, then sat in a little booth by the window.

"Can you make him disappear?" Crank barely waited until I slid into my seat.

I had to suppress a shudder at his words. "What do you mean?"

He rolled his eyes. "Can you make it look like he went back to his momma? End his case, or whatever it is you do?"

I thought about that. "Well, yes, but—"

"Then that's what we do." He turned to Jimmy. "You got any relatives? If you could go live with anyone, who would it be?"

Jimmy considered for a long moment. "You. None of the relatives would take me. They all said I'm a bad seed."

Crank growled just as the waitress arrived with our food, but he stayed quiet while she put everything on the table. "Kid, you don't know me. I might be worse than the people at that home."

The ketchup bottle, nearly empty, refused to give up as much as Jimmy wanted, so he set it back on the table with a thump. "No you're not. I don't take up much space, and I don't eat a lot. I can even be quiet. And I can work."

Crank's gaze met mine, a storm of emotion flashing in the shadowed depths. "Kid—"

"You won't even know I'm there. I promise." The desperation in Jimmy's tone brought tears to my eyes. This poor child felt so unwanted by those who were supposed to care for him, he would rather trust a stranger not to hurt him.

Crank sighed, then raised a hand to signal the waitress. "Let me get another bottle of ketchup. And I need to borrow your pen." He accepted the pen while the woman rushed off to bring the ketchup. "You take a napkin there, and you write down your momma's name, address, phone number, any and everything you know."

Fear flickered in Jimmy's face for just a moment as he took the pen, and started to print carefully on the napkin. Without a word, he passed it back to Crank. The waitress returned, and Cranked traded her the pen for the fresh bottle, and helped Jimmy get more onto his plate.

I couldn't wait any longer. "What are you doing, Crank?"

Instead of replying, he tapped out a quick text, then took a photo of the napkin, and sent it as well. "Don't worry. Nothing sketchy." We ate in silence for a few minutes, before his phone beeped with a return text. He glanced at the screen. "I was thinking, you want to go back to Chancey's for a couple of days? Until you get everything settled here so we can head back to Kentucky?"

"What about..." I gestured vaguely toward Jimmy.

"Being handled. And that's a great place for a kid to spend a few days."

Excitement fluttered through me at the prospect of spending more time with Chancey. It would also give me time to figure out how to talk to my parents. "I'd like that."

"Good. Now where the fuck do people get clothes and shit for kids?"

I sputtered laughter. "The mall? I don't know, but that's probably a good place to start."

Crank just nodded, and went back to eating as if deep in thought. Jimmy's hero worship already showed in the way he subtly mimicked Crank, from his posture, to where he placed his drink on the table. Whatever Crank had in mind, I prayed it didn't break this child's heart any worse than it already was.

We finished, and left the diner, and Crank asked directions to the nearest mall. The next hour and a half passed in a haze of male frustration, as Crank listed the items he wanted to purchase for Jimmy, and they both grumped about having to choose. Finally, though, we left the mall intact, with a handful of bags containing what Crank considered the essentials for a boy Jimmy's age. At least he relented on the steel-toed boots, and let us pick a pair of nice sneakers, too.

Jimmy chattered ceaselessly the entire drive back to Chancey's place, although he started pausing for yawns in the last few miles. His excitement proved contagious, causing Crank to grin often. I seemed alone in the concern gnawing at my mind. Jimmy certainly wasn't worried. Now that Crank had taken over, he acted as a boy his age should, and trusted that his hero would take care of him. I wished I could share that trust. Unfortunately, I knew too much about how the real world worked.

We drove up by Chancey's house, and I had to admit, I was relieved to see lights on, and the place looking normal. I rushed up onto the porch and knocked, waiting impatiently.

A long moment later, Chancey swung the door open, face wreathed in smiles. "You came back!" The force of her hug nearly knocked me over. "Oh my God, I'm so glad to see you!" She chattered on, carelessly waving Crank to help himself when he mentioned that we needed rooms.

As soon as he and Jimmy disappeared upstairs, she tugged my hand, leading me to the kitchen. I paused in the door, a little surprised to see Runner leaning against her counter. He acknowledged me with a nod, but his gaze returned immediately to Chancey.

"Runner said he thought you'd show up soon. I thought he was crazy. Figured Crank had hauled you off to a cave somewhere." She laughed again. "Oh, you have to see pictures of the baby! She's beautiful." She grabbed her cell phone and started flicking photos in front of me, explaining each one. "My sister is so happy, just over the moon." Despite the smiles, I detected a hint of sadness in the words.

"And what about you?"

She lifted a shoulder a little, still smiling. "I'm really good. Glad to have my bladder back, for one thing." Sorrow flitted over her face. "I really have to make a decision, though. I don't think I can handle staying here, at least for a while.

Giving the baby back was harder than I thought."

My mind started to race. Would she consider Kentucky? Would Crank's friends welcome her? Because the prospect of a familiar face in the new surroundings sounded like a great idea.

CHAPTER 30

Crank:

That kid fucking got to me. If my crazy scheme didn't pan out, I had no clue what to do, but I'd be fucked if I left him there for some other sonofabitch to beat on. Sarah thought I'd lost it, and maybe I had. But I followed my instincts mostly, and they told me this was a good kid, but he needed help, badly. I intended to give.

The tenth time I checked for a new text, Sarah busted me. "Waiting for something?"

"I am." I knew she wanted details, or at least a hint, but I couldn't do that yet. Just saying it out loud might ruin it all. So she would have to wait. I looked around for a distraction, and spotted a jaw-cracking yawn from Jimmy. "Hey, kid, let's get you settled upstairs. You had a busy day."

Obstinate little shit thought about arguing, but another yawn changed his mind. "Okay. I am a little tired."

I went up with him, waited while he brushed his teeth and changed into a pair of loose shorts. He slid into the bed, and I pulled the covers over him, even though he was perfectly capable of doing it himself. "You need me, you holler, okay? Even if it's a bad dream, or just nerves. I'm a light sleeper, so I'll hear you." I paused a moment. "I might have to go out for a minute, but if I do, Sarah will be here, and she'll help you, too. So just holler."

He gave a serious nod. "I will. Thanks, Crank. This is the

best day of my life." He kind of snuggled into the pillow, closed his eyes, and just like that, he was out.

Good thing, too. I couldn't tell him this might be only temporary. Deep in thought, I headed back down to where Sarah and the others chatted in the kitchen. She looked up the moment I came in, but I avoided her gaze and detoured to the fridge for a bottle of water.

Her soft voice cut through it all as soon as I sat down. "Crank, honey, what are you doing?"

I started to answer, but my phone buzzed. A single word. *'Done'*. The grin nearly cracked my face. "Looks like I'm getting a kid."

Confusion wrinkled her forehead, while Chancey and Runner looked from me to her. "What do you mean? You can't just take him home with you like a stray puppy."

I scowled, forgetting for a minute that she only wanted what was best, for both me and the kid. "His momma just signed custody over to me. It'll get entered at court tomorrow."

Her jaw fell. "H-how did you..."

"Doesn't matter. Only fucking thing that matters is that he's safe now." Fear hit me like a brick. "You with me on this?" I hadn't even fucking considered how she might see it.

She smiled. "I'm very with you!" She threw her arms around my neck. "You're sure it'll all work out?"

"Anything can happen, of course, but yeah, I'm fucking sure. My brothers are taking care of shit for me. By the time you wrap up here and get ready to go, it'll all be taken care of, nice and legal." Relief thudded through my veins.

"Go?" Chancey sounded alarmed. "Where are you going?" Damn, she looked like some bastard just pulled the lifeline from her hands.

The glance Sarah sent me as she returned to her seat

spoke volumes. "I'm going back to Kentucky with Crank. My life is wherever he is."

"Oh. I sorta thought...Well, I don't really know what I thought. Maybe I can come visit you sometime." She rose and went to busy herself at the sink, wiping down things that already sparkled. Sarah went to her, leaving Runner and me sitting there.

He dropped his phone to the table. "You'd think I was a fucking invalid, or something."

"Come again?" Apparently I'd missed something.

"Dad and all the others keep asking if I'm okay. Think I'm going to go Nomad for a while, get some fresh air."

Well, that made sense. "Might be a good idea. You ever get to Kentucky, come by. The Raiders will make you welcome."

His chair scraped the floor as he shoved back all of a sudden. "Hey, Chancey, what kind of plans you got for the next couple weeks?"

She and Sarah turned to stare at him like he'd sprouted another head. "Nothing. Why?"

"You want to take a little trip with me? Check out the scenery in Kentucky?"

Huh. I hadn't seen that fucking coming. A new text came and I glanced at my phone once more. "While y'all figure out the details, I got some business to attend to." I stood and kissed Sarah. "I'll be back as soon as I can. Keep an ear out for Jimmy. Wouldn't surprise me if the kid had nightmares."

A small worried frown creased her brow. "Is everything okay?"

"Never better." I smiled and kissed her again. "Just need to settle a couple of things up so we can focus on getting home." I leaned closer, so only she could hear. "Talk her into this. It'll be good for you, too."

She hugged me close, clearly excited. "Thank you, Crank."

If Runner suspected anything, he ignored it, paying no attention beyond a lifted hand as I left. The drive to Betty Blue's went uneventfully, the darkened streets nearly empty. I parked and went inside, waiting for a Prospect to lead me back to the club's area. As intimidating as that first meeting with them was, this was entirely new fucking territory.

At first I thought they had dimmed the lights, or some shit, but as I rounded the last pallet and came into the open space, I realized they hadn't bothered with electric lights. Instead, a campfire provided the flickering illumination. What I had assumed to be a solid roof seemed to have been drawn back, opening the entire area to the sky above. Interesting.

I paused, taking everything in. The Ghost Walkers stood around, some talking quietly, others sprawled on the ground. They had shed the trappings of civilization this time, faces streaked with paint, and regular clothing replaced by traditional.

My skin prickled. This shit felt like accidentally stepping into a war camp, with blood-thirsty warriors planning the death and destruction of their enemy. I fucking filed that away to fill Kellen in. These motherfuckers would have a huge psychological advantage in a club war. We needed them on our side, if possible.

Off to one side, a cluster of men caught my attention. They huddled close together, and a closer look showed why. More than a dozen prisoners, all bound hand and foot, were tethered close together, guarded by a pair of vicious looking dogs.

"I hope you don't mind, I decided to combine our

business with tradition." Fergus' voice right behind my shoulder startled me, but I managed to keep still.

"Don't mind at all. Ready to get started? I got shit to get back to."

White teeth flashed in the black paint covering the lower half of his face. "Sounds good to me." He raised a hand and all his men rose to their feet and fell silent. "Before we get on to business, we have some entertainment tonight. These white men are all child molesters. They have committed horrible crimes, some of them against our own. We will have vengeance for all their victims." He nodded to the other side of the room, and a low, ominous throbbing noise filled the air.

About the time I identified the sound as a drum, Fergus continued.

He turned to the prisoners. "The drums will carry your screams to your victims, and they will laugh with your suffering." One of the sick bastards retched at the thought. Fergus laughed and turned to me. "I hope your stomach is not weak, my friend."

I grinned. "Is Lanea here?"

He nodded. "Of course. Two of these men will feel the bite of her blades tonight."

"Good. If it's okay with you, I'd like to help with that one over there." I pointed to the man from the foster home. "I need information from Sennit about any other connections, and I think what I have planned will encourage him to talk."

Fergus shrugged. "Sure. Have fun. But when your methods don't work, one of my men will take over."

"I think they'll be able to save their talents for other things."

He waved Lanea over, and I stepped aside with her to explain quickly what I had in mind. The more I talked, the

more she smiled. When we were ready, she called for the man
to be brought over by the fire.

He screamed and begged, struggling against the pair
who dragged him between them until the rope around his
ankles was secured to a post, while the one holding his wrists
wrapped around another. When the ends of the ropes were
pulled abruptly, he fell so his head struck the floor with a dull
thud. I hoped they hadn't knocked his ass out.

At Fergus' nod, I went forward with Lanea. I laid my cut
over a chair not far away, and shed my t-shirt. Ready, I turned
to where Sennit and the others looked on in dread. "Sennit, this
one is for you. Unless you give my friends here all the fucking
information they want, you'll get Hell Fire, too."

Suddenly, the fucking idiot got brave. "I remember you.
You're the dumb thug that was sniffing around after Sarah
Channing. You better stay with your own kind. She'll be mine
before this is settled."

I shoved the anger back. "Nah, she's damaged goods,
considering my kid is already in her belly." I let that one sink
in, more than half wishing it were true, while I accepted the
two-foot piece of re-bar one of Fergus' men brought. "Now,
Hell Fire starts with this right here." I laid the steel in the edge
of the fire.

The man stretched between the posts groaned in fear,
while Sennit laughed. "A few burns? That's the best you can
do?"

I stayed silent, just nodded to Lanea. Together, we cut
the man's clothing away until he lay naked before the crowd.
By the time we finished, the steel was hot. I picked two of the
observers at random. "You, and you. Cut the ropes on his feet.
Pull his legs apart, and bring his knees to his chest. You'll have
to lean on him once this gets started, so be ready."

The men glanced doubtfully at one another, but shrugged and followed orders.

Lanea gave a blood-thirsty grin. "If he's too much for you, I can hamstring him. He won't be able to fight then. He'll have to just lay back and enjoy it, like he told me to do."

I considered briefly. It drastically raised the psychological stakes. "Good idea. I like it. Then besides shitting in a bag the rest of his life, if he's lucky enough to live that long, he won't be doing a lot of walking either."

At my nod, Lanea went forward. Her blade flashed in the firelight as it dipped into the man's flesh, severing first one hamstring, then the other. The man's screams filled the air, echoing off the steel walls until it seemed like a hundred men being tortured.

Finally, the noise subsided a little, and I pulled on my leather gloves, grabbed the cool end of the re-bar, and moved toward him. Pausing for a just a second, I gestured to Sennit with the steel. "Just in case you hadn't guessed, this goes up his ass. You see why we call it Hell Fire." The glowing tip of the metal held every man in the place mesmerized. Taking my time, I lined up, then gave a quick shove, careful not to go too deep.

The man screamed until he lost consciousness, just like they always did.

Fergus looked at me closely. "Damn. I didn't think a white man could teach a Plains warrior anything about torture. I stand corrected."

I grinned back. "Well, hang on, because we're just getting started."

EPILOGUE

Crank:

I had to admit to being a little shocked when Sennit needed no further encouragement to talk after the re-bar up the bastard's ass. Of course, he got plenty more. As soon as he said he would talk, I stepped back, and let Lanea and Fergus' men do whatever they needed. I was satisfied. I'd terrorized the motherfucker as badly as he scared Sarah. The only thing I needed was to get back to my woman.

The following day, I didn't bother giving her details, but I was pretty sure Sarah knew at least the gist of what happened in the back of that bakery. She didn't ask for details, either, but I got the feeling she took comfort in knowing the lengths I was prepared to go to for her. As long as she felt safe again, the rest didn't matter.

I kept my head down and did whatever I could to make the whole thing easier for her, and spent time with Jimmy. He really was a good kid, but he needed guidance. The more I learned about his past, the more anger simmered in my blood. I needed to pay his bitch mother a visit before long.

Sarah:

Wrapping up my life took shockingly little time. I turned my resignation in with my reports, and found almost no red-tape attached. For some reason, Sennit cooperated fully with authorities, giving them the identities of several other pedophiles and confessing to his own part in the whole thing. Most of the others from the motel that day chose to cooperate, as well. I was pretty sure Crank and Fergus had something to do with their willingness to be so helpful, but I didn't care. The only thing that mattered to me was having it ended.

The day Mom and Dad came back from their cruise, I asked them to meet me for dinner at their favorite restaurant. I wanted Jimmy to come with us, but he wanted to stay at Chancey's. He and Runner had struck up a friendship that seemed good for both of them, so Crank agreed.

Crank and I reached the quiet little Italian place first, and had the hostess show us to the table to wait. By my reasoning, my parents could hardly pitch a fit in public when they met Crank. It felt like an insurance policy, especially since I had no real clue how he would react to the various names they might call him.

By the time they arrived, my napkin lay in shreds on the table in front of me. "Sarah, you didn't say you were bringing a friend." Mom leaned in for a hug. "Last minute?" Her gaze flicked in Crank's direction and her eyes widened subtly.

Crank stood, offered his hand, and introduced himself by his real name. He even managed not to growl when my mother wiped her hand after touching his. "Sarah's told me a lot about the two of you."

My dad's brows dropped a little. "Shocking, since she hasn't said a word to us about you."

"Well, sir, there's a reason for that." Crank glanced toward me.

"Mom, you remember what I told you about work? Sennit?"

She nodded as the waiter arrived to take our orders.

As soon as he left, I continued. "Crank kept me safe

during that, and made sure Sennit and his friends were brought to justice."

Well, that did it. Mom suddenly turned all smiles. "Oh, you're the FBI Agent? You should have said so. I must say, your appearance is very deceptive, but I suppose you have to blend in with the criminals." She chattered on, while Dad watched Crank's reactions.

"Merrin, I don't think he's FBI." Dad's pronouncement brought silence to the table.

Crank nodded. "No, sir, I'm not. I'm also not quite the low-life you thought when we met either. The part you need to know is that I love Sarah more than life, and I have the skills and resources to keep her safe, and give her the kind of life she deserves."

Dad sneered. "As what? A crack whore? If you actually love her, you'll walk out of here right now and never look back."

Crank popped his knuckles under the table, a nervous gesture I'd never seen from him before. The grin he gave was one I had come to recognize as a warning, more like a snarl. "Actually, she could do anything she wants, including continue her work with kids. But the thing is, she chooses to make her life with me. We're leaving for Kentucky tomorrow. You're welcome to visit, of course, but I won't tolerate my family being judged." His voice softened a little. "I'll take good care of her, sir, and if for some reason I can't, my brothers will."

Mom cleared her throat, and turned to me. "We're so happy for you, Sarah!"

Did I just walk into the Twilight Zone? "Okay, who are you, and what have you done with my mother?"

She just laughed. "He isn't what we would have chosen for you, of course. But we've known for a long time you weren't cut out for the kind of man to be deterred by your father's scowl."

Just like that, the tension was gone. We had a good meal, talking and laughing as my parents became acquainted with Crank. By the time we finished dessert, they had even started calling him by that name, instead of his real one.

We spent that night in my childhood room at my parents' home, planning to pack a few things and make an early start the next morning. Crank locked the door, and settled his large frame onto the ruffly bedspread.

I raised up on my elbow, smiling down at him. "This isn't awkward at all."

His smile practically curled my toes. "Not at all. I hope your folks are sound sleepers."

Were they? I didn't know. "Why?"

"If not, they're going to hear us making love." He quirked one eyebrow. "But then, they might learn a thing or two."

"Oh, my God!" I tried to muffle my laughter against his chest. Then embarrassment set in. "No, I'll go to the guest room. I can't believe Mom didn't insist on that to begin with."

He brushed my hair back. "Hey, stop worrying. They want you happy and safe, nothing more. If you'd rather not, we'll wait. I'm not going to insist, and embarrass you like that."

When he said sweet things like that, how could I resist? "Maybe we could just be really quiet?"

He shifted, turning toward me, and the bed groaned in protest.

"Sarah? Honey, did you need something?" Mom's voice carried far too easily in the quiet house.

I laughed. "No, Mom, we're good. But, uh, you might rest better with the TV on, or something."

My dad's quiet laughter cut off abruptly as the TV blared some late night comedy routine.

I leaned in to kiss Crank. "Now, where were we?"

"I don't know about you, but I was about to tell you how much I love you." He met my kiss, and deepened it. He turned carefully to bring me on top of him, and for the first time, he let me help roll on the condom, hissing as I touched him. "I can't wait to get home and get the all-clear, so we don't have to worry with these damn things anymore."

I rose over him and guided him into position. "I can't either. Maybe we'll get rid of the birth control pills then, too."

The force of his thrust drove a loud gasp from me. So much for our intentions to stay quiet.

***

Everything looked so different here, but Crank drove too quickly for me to take much of it in. As soon as our plane landed, he had shuffled Jimmy and me off to get our luggage, and then to the parking garage. Runner and Chancey decided to drive from Oklahoma, so I had to face it all alone.

I consoled myself with reminders that I had already met some of Crank's friends, and they would be there. It wasn't like going to a place where I didn't know a single soul. And I had Jimmy to keep me busy, too. We had to get him all registered for school and ready to go.

When Crank turned the car down a dirt road, my lungs refused to draw in air quickly enough, and my heart tried to jump away. Behind me, Jimmy chattered on, oblivious, having spotted animals in a field nearby.

Crank reached over and took my hand. "Breathe, Sarah. It's okay." He parked the car in front of a sprawling house with a yard full of people. "They're going to love you as much as I do."

He got out and came around to open my door, and took my arm while I got out. Cheers erupted all around us, and I nearly dove back inside the car.

"Everyone, shut the fuck up!" He waited a moment for silence to settle over the crowd. "This is Sarah. She's my ol' lady. And this is Jimmy, and he's my kid now."

More cheering, and finally, I spotted a familiar face. Cherry. "Well, Crank, I'm glad to see you got your head outta your ass. We missed your handsome face around here." She smacked his shoulder, then turned me. "Welcome to the Hell Raiders, Sarah."

THE END

If you liked Crank's Rescue, you might also like my other books:

Hell Raiders MC Romance Series

Kellen's Redemption (Hell Raiders MC Book #1)

Dixon's Resurrection (Hell Raiders MC Book #2)

Trip's Retribution (Hell Raiders MC Book #3)

Prizefight (Hell Raiders MC Book #4

Fabio's Remorse (Hell Raiders MC Book #5)

Hunted Love Series

Big Game: Hunted Love #1

Bounty: Hunted Love #2

Captured: Hunted Love #3

Unwanted Soldiers Series

Target: Unwanted Soldiers #1

Ride Series – Co Written with Ashley Wheels

Ride It Out

If you'd like to stay up to date on what I'm working on,

- Visit my website, www.adenlowe.com
- Join my Facebook Group, The Lowe-Down for exclusive snippets, early looks, members only giveaways, and lots of fun.

Made in the USA
Columbia, SC
21 July 2017